Evangeline's Ghost

C. A. Pack

This is a work of fiction. The characters, incidents, and dialogue are products of the author's imagination and are not to be construed as real. Any resemblance to actual events or persons, living or dead, is entirely coincidental. The exceptions to the preceding are President Harry and First Lady Bess Truman, Secret Service chief Frank Wilson, and actor Ethel Merman, who are historical figures. Their itineraries mentioned in this book are historically accurate. All other material is the product of the author's imagination.

Published by Artiqua Press

175 Maple Avenue, Ste. 3A, Westbury, NY 11590

www.ArtiquaPress.com

EVANGELINE'S GHOST

ISBN: 0983572364

ISBN-13:978-0983572367

DEDICATION

I dedicate *Evangeline's Ghost* to all the spirits who live on in my heart: Ryan Michael, Patsy Cosmos, Natalie Marie, Carmelo, Alfia and Mal.

CHAPTER ONE

Nuremberg, Germany
1946

VICTORIA MÉLIÈS LINGERED IN A HALF-DREAM HAZE for as long as she dared. She did not want to leave the comfort of the eiderdown feather bed, but a slender shaft of sunlight sliced across the silky duvet under which she sought refuge, and she knew it was time to face the masses.

She looked over her notes for the deposition she planned to give later that morning, against a man believed to be a Nazi war criminal. Her employer, MI6, had argued that open testimony during the Nuremberg trials would force her to reveal her identity and would compromise her safety. Instead, her deposition would be taken in secrecy using her code name: Evangeline.

She dressed carefully. Her beauty often diverted attention away from the importance of her words. She pulled her hair back in a severe chignon, covered the rest of her crowning glory with a brown felt hat, and wore a modest suit.

The butterflies in her stomach influenced her decision to skip breakfast. She could always make up for it later with a generous portion of Wiener schnitzel at the beer garden around the corner.

She waited for a car to pick her up. Each minute felt like an hour. She paced the lobby of her hotel, hating every step she took, but knowing all the while she could not stop the apprehension that enveloped her.

The lobby was intimate and just the slightest bit shabby. The blue-and-gold carpeting underfoot appeared threadbare in places, the wood-paneled walls lacked luster, and the marble that topped the reception desk had a crack running through the center of it. But even though the hotel had seen better days, it more than made up for its worn-out appearance with cleanliness and comfort. She smiled at the thought of the feather bed. She would enjoy going to sleep that evening, but first, she needed to get through the day.

Victoria berated herself for having jangled nerves. *It's not like I'm appearing at the Palace of Justice with a fabricated story I need to make everyone believe. I'm going to tell the truth about an incident involving a Nazi official.* Still, she could not shake the anxiety she felt.

A sleek black car pulled up in front of the hotel. Even before a British commander emerged, she knew the car was for her. She nodded at the officer when he entered the lobby, and walked out ahead of him with her head bent toward the ground.

As soon as she entered the Mercedes Benz sedan, a British councilor began advising her. "Only use your code name. Even if asked directly, do not state your real name. Do not give out information other than the code names of your colleagues. Do not give out your address, birth date, or any other personal information. Simply state the steps you took to prevent Heinz Bruchman from undermining an Allied invasion plan. And by all means, don't offer any information other than what you're directly questioned about. Your feelings are not relevant. Only divulge what you witnessed with your own eyes and ears."

"I feel like I'm the person on trial—rather than Bruchman."

"To repeat what I just said, your feelings are not relevant."

The Palace of Justice was a massive cream-colored edifice with a vivid red roof. Niches filled with stone statuary punctuated the top of the building. The impressive walls concealed not only courtrooms and offices, but also a prison. It was one of the few buildings of its size in the area to survive WWII nearly intact. It had been chosen for the trials because Nuremberg was in Allied territory and had been the site of numerous Nazi rallies. Some called it poetic justice.

"We will not be going to courtroom 600," the councilor explained. "Even though that's the main courtroom, we have been directed to a smaller office because of the secrecy of your testimony. I've been there before. It's a simple room overlooking an interior courtyard. It's across from the prison wing. Do not allow the setting to undermine your duty. You are testifying on behalf of the British government."

His attempts to put her at ease made her more

nervous. She dropped her handbag as she got out of the car. The councilor and her military escort continued toward the building while she stooped to retrieve her purse. She sighed as she stood up, feeling clumsy and foolish.

A shot rang out, disorienting her. She immediately forgot the councilor's advice.

CHAPTER TWO

Pearly Gates

"Next."

The tall, bald man with the hooked nose looked directly at her.

"Me?"

"Yes, you. Name?"

"Victoria Méliès."

"That's not right."

"Well, of course it is. I know my own name."

"I've got your file right here and it says your name is Evangeline."

"That's my code name."

"Regardless, forevermore, you'll be known as Evangeline."

"No. You don't understand. It's a code name, so no one will connect me with Evangeline."

He stamped the top of her file. "You only have

one name here, and it's Evangeline. Line three. Next."

She turned to look where he was pointing. Hundreds of people waited in the next line. "That will take forever."

He shooed her away with a flutter of his hand. "You've got forever. Trust me."

Line three snaked all around the brightly lit and expansive space. She found the end of it and took her position behind a young man in a U.S. Army uniform. He turned to her. "Do you know what we're doing here?"

"I'm wondering if this is a hospital," she answered. "I remember getting a headache. And now I'm here." Her voice trailed off as she looked at the soldier more closely. He had a hole in his chest the size of her fist. "What happened?" she whispered, never taking her eyes from his wound.

He looked confused. He felt the edges of the gaping hole and his face filled with fear. He looked back at Evangeline but couldn't form the words to answer her.

She pushed her hair back from her face and he gasped. "What is it?" she asked.

He just stared at her.

She lifted her hand to her head. Something wasn't right. Evangeline looked for her mirror, but she had no handbag. She searched the area around her. How could this be? She had never gone anywhere without a handbag. How would she pay for a taxi? What if she needed a handkerchief? What if she were attacked? Her *gun* was in her handbag.

She left the line and went back to speak to the tall, bald man with the hooked nose. After being ignored by him for what she considered too long a time, she butted in. "I seem to have lost my handbag. Is there a place to retrieve lost items around here?"

"You're supposed to be on line three."

"I was, but I can't find my handbag."

"You don't need one," he answered abruptly.

"But I do. There's something wrong with the side of my head and I want to see what it is. My mirror is in my handbag."

"Mirrors are a symbol of vanity."

"And all my money is in there."

"Money is a sign of greed. Get back in line."

"No. You don't understand. I have to see what's wrong with me." She tried not to sound hysterical, but her voice rose in pitch and volume.

"You don't understand. You don't understand," he mimicked. "Is that the only thing you know how to say?"

Evangeline frowned. "Why are you being so rude to me?"

"Okay," he continued, reaching toward her and turning over his hand. The tiny gold mirror she carried in her bag was sitting in his palm.

She snatched it away. "You have my handbag. I want it back this instant."

Saint Peter sighed. "I don't have your handbag."

"You have my *mirror*," she retorted.

"No. *You* have your mirror," he said, looking at her hand. "Now, go away."

"I demand to see your superior."

"I'd like to see him myself. I agreed to be the bishop of Rome. Everyone said 'nice work if you can get it.' But before I knew it, they hung me upside down, and bing-bang-boom, they crucified me. And now I'm here, shepherding his flock. I'm thinking you're one of the black sheep."

"I beg your pardon?"

"Look in the mirror."

Evangeline surveyed her reflection. She pushed her hair back. She had a hole in her temple big enough to stick a cigar in. She fainted, but as soon as she went down she felt something pull her back up.

"There's no fainting here. You're dead, Evangeline. For a spy, you've got very little gumption. Now get back in line for Purgatory, or I'll send you to Limbo instead. You wouldn't like it there. No one does."

"I can't be dead. I've got too much I still need to do."

"Don't we all. You're lucky I didn't send you straight to Hell. You've assassinated quite a few people. And you lie like a rug. But you have a good heart. Some of the people you killed were honest mistakes. Others truly deserved to die. But one of the bad guys got you before you could get him. Or was it her? I can't recall."

"Shot me," she said quizzically. "You mean intentionally? I was murdered?"

"Please," he said with disgust, "don't tell me you want to go back and avenge your death. There are too many ghosts in the ether already, and revenge—I might point out—is a sin."

"But I need to know what happened."

"Oh, for crying out loud, all you secret agents are the same. You think you're so smart. But you're not, you know, or you wouldn't be here making my death miserable."

"I demand—"

"Stop with the demands, already. You want to go back? Good, I'll send you back. But you're going to languish there until you find your killer. I was being nice. I was trying to give you some peace of mind. Purgatory isn't Heaven, but we can't all stay at the Five-Star Hotel."

"I wish I could remember …" Her voice trailed off.

"And now you want special favors?"

"I think I was in Germany."

The man looked up. The heavens above changed to a warm golden hue, and they heard the herald of trumpets followed by the sweet sigh of violins.

"Well, Evangeline, this must be your lucky day."

CHAPTER THREE

New York, New York
1946

A FLOOD OF MEMORIES CARRIED HER INTO THE PAST, BUT the jolt of the gunshot that killed her brought Evangeline back to the present. She examined the bullet hole with her fingers.

Saint Peter could see the change in her. "I knew you weren't going to like it."

"Like it? Somebody shot me."

"Well, yes, I believe we established that point *before* you decided to relive the horror."

"I've got to find out who did it. You have to send me back."

"If you go back, you'll have to stay until you bring your killer to justice."

"Agreed."

"It's not what you're used to …"

"Just send me back," she said more emphatically.

Saint Peter lifted both his palms to heaven and looked up. Instead of golden light and sweet music, the Pearly Gates shook as a bolt of lightning electrified the air.

Evangeline found herself standing inside the four-story ballroom of the Waldorf Astoria hotel in Manhattan. She watched for a moment as elegantly dressed couples swirled across the dance floor, then noticed her clothing had changed. She looked exquisite in vintage Chanel, the same gown she had worn to an affair in this ballroom, years before. Her honey-blond hair fell in a long swoop over one shoulder. She lifted her hand automatically, feeling for her mother's comb. The diamond-studded hair ornament had been her mother's favorite, and Evangeline wept when her mother presented it to her on her eighteenth birthday.

She stood on a small balcony that jutted out over the ballroom floor and surveyed the people who stood chatting below her. They wore bespoke clothing and elaborate jewelry and blended beautifully with the red, gold, and cream décor that gave the ballroom its regal appearance. She recognized many of the guests. They were the crème de la crème of New York and international society, and they were doing what they did best—socializing with their peers.

Evangeline inhaled the aroma of braised pheasant and asparagus, which lingered in the air. She may have died, but her olfactory glands were alive and kicking, and she wondered if she could still enjoy the taste of food. She smiled as she continued watching the guests mingle while waiting for dessert to be served.

A couple sat down at the table next to her. She smiled as she greeted them. "Good evening." They didn't respond. "Excuse me," she continued, "do you have the time?" They continued to ignore her. A waiter carrying a tray filled with desserts reached through her and placed one on the table. She whirled around, her eyes wide, as she realized that for these people, she didn't exist.

A raven-haired socialite who looked vaguely familiar caught her eye. Evangeline descended to the main floor to get a better look, amazed at how easily she could move about.

The woman wore gold wire-rimmed eyeglasses shaped like octagons. She carried a jewel-encrusted cigarette holder that was half as long as her opera-gloved arm and her low-cut beaded black gown snugly hugged every curve and then some. Bright red toenails peeked out from open-toed shoes.

As soon as she opened her mouth, the mystery surrounding her identity ended. Evangeline immediately recognized her nemesis's low-class, high-class accent.

Bunny Stanton.

Bunny had been a thorn in Evangeline's corporeal side during some of her previous missions, including the one that resulted in her becoming an agent for MI6. Bunny had killed two people Evangeline was fond of, and nearly killed Evangeline in the summer of '36 by rigging a grenade to explode when she entered her hotel suite. But the blast killed another agent instead—Nigel Townsend—who had volunteered to retrieve Evangeline's passport from her room, so she could leave the country undetected.

Evangeline quickly stepped back so Bunny

wouldn't see her and then stopped. Of course, Bunny couldn't see her. No one could.

Evangeline had completed seven successful operations for the Crown before being murdered. Now, she was cursed to roam her old haunts looking for her killer.

She heard a heavenly groan.

All right. Maybe *cursed* wasn't exactly the right word, considering she had demanded to be returned to earth. But she was miffed. *I'm dead and Bunny isn't and that's not fair considering Bunny killed Nigel.*

Besides, even if Evangeline found the person responsible for her death, Saint Peter said she would not be able to escape the ether that bound her to earth until she brought her murderer to justice.

That's where things could get tricky. She now knew most people couldn't see her, and she was pretty sure it would limit her ability to communicate. She moaned, not exactly sure how she would solve the mystery surrounding her death, or even if she could. But she would die trying, or something like that.

Nigel had been killed entering the Presidential Suite. Her suite. She suddenly wanted to go there and see where the devastating blast had occurred—something she had never wanted to do in life. She had been thinking about Nigel a lot lately, although she couldn't explain why.

As soon as she envisioned the room where Nigel had met his maker, she was transported there. She lingered out in the hallway, working up the courage to go inside, but not for long. The choice was taken away from her when a powerful force enveloped Evangeline and dragged her inside the suite.

EG

CHAPTER FOUR

Bunny Stanton felt a sudden chill and wished she hadn't allowed the hotel's coat-check girl to talk her into relinquishing her mink stole. Her cousin, an actress, had given it to her as a goodbye present to get Bunny away from her husband and out of her life.

"Are you okay?" Hutchinson Smythe voiced his concern when Bunny faltered mid-sentence. He was one of several men listening to her tale of how she defied her aristocratic family to become an actress.

The icy presence that had caused her to momentarily freeze, left as quickly as it had arrived, and Bunny continued with her story. She smiled, glad that Hutchinson had inquired about her well-being. It meant he was interested, and she never ignored a good-looking multimillionaire industrialist, especially when he showed concern for her. Her eyes glowed when he laughed at the witticism she used to end her story. "Hutchinson, darling, would you mind terribly getting me another glass of pink champagne?"

He seemed reluctant to leave her side, but did her bidding, and when he returned she favored him with all her attention, much to the chagrin of the other men hoping to win her over. Hutch, as his friends called him, owned mines, mills, and media companies, and Bunny set her sights on becoming Mrs. Hutchinson Smythe.

Bunny had met Hutch at a private party at the Stork Club. He didn't know she had crashed the event and she told him she was a friend of the host. He said he didn't know the host very well, and Bunny felt safe in her lie.

Now she had "run into" him again at a gala birthday party for the head of one of America's wealthiest families. She wasn't on the guest list, but if she wanted to find a rich husband, she had to play in his playground. And it wasn't below Bunny to crash a party if she thought it might help feather her nest.

She had no problem getting in. All she had to do was look the part and act like she belonged. And while her name might not be found among the bright lights of Broadway, she was an accomplished actress when it came to subterfuge and obfuscation. It paid off. A ring of debonair men, whose hearts she would happily break, completely surrounded her.

The wait staff in the ballroom began serving dessert, and Hutch steered Bunny toward his table, which was prominently placed. It's what she had hoped he would do, otherwise, she would have been forced to sit on an upper balcony behind a support pole. It was the only seat available, and she knew it was her own fault. She had arrived too late to bluff her way into a better position.

Bunny toyed with her Floating Island. She had been about to suggest an alternative to dessert, but Hutch dug into his serving with such gusto that she held back.

"I'm not one for French food, but I've got to commend the French for creating this particular confection. I don't know what I like better, the meringue or the custard, but when I like something, I've got to have it immediately."

"Well, one of these days I'll just have to cook dinner for you and make your favorite dessert."

He picked up each of her hands in his own and kissed them in succession. "That sounds like a wonderful idea."

After he scraped the last bit of meringue from his plate, Bunny placed her hand on his sleeve. "Dance with me, Hutchinson."

"I'd be glad to." He led her to the center of the room and waltzed her across the highly polished dance floor.

Yes. Being Mrs. Hutchinson Smythe would be very nice indeed.

Evangeline swayed. Her forced passage through the door of the Presidential Suite was not as exhilarating as thinking about being someplace and immediately being transported there. She wasn't ready to enter the suite, and getting yanked inside, against her will, had been disquieting.

"Evangeline, are you all right?" She recognized

the voice and focused her vision on the speaker. "Nigel." She relaxed her shoulders. "I hoped you'd be here."

Their sometimes-strained relationship from a decade before, no longer existed. Now, Evangeline and Nigel talked like long lost lovers trying to reestablish their connection.

"I keep waiting for my murderer to return to the scene of the crime," Nigel explained. "But from what I can see, none of the hundreds of people who have checked into this room over the years seems responsible for my death."

"Maybe not, but I'm pretty sure the culprit is in the ballroom, right now."

"What makes you so certain?"

"Because the War Office, along with its American counterpart, investigated your death and determined Bunny Stanton planted the grenade that caused it."

"Bunny? A grenade? Where would Bunny get a grenade?"

"A place called Canal Street. I believe the exact location has been shuttered since then."

Over the next few hours, Evangeline told Nigel what she knew about his death and all about the conclusion of the mission they had been on together. She then brought him up to date on what she had been doing ever since.

"Evangeline, you never cease to amaze me."

"Wait."

"What's the matter?"

"You never, in your life, called me Evangeline. You didn't learn my code name until the day you died.

Yet that's what you're calling me now. Why?"

"Because that's what you're now known as."

"Yes. But how do *you* know that?"

"It's kind of a *Collective* thing. I just know it."

"What does that mean?"

"Look, Evie, you're new—"

"Evie? Now it's Evie?"

"It's an endearment." He smiled at her. "I was always rather taken with you."

"You never showed it."

"I was assigned to protect you on a mission. At first I intended to seduce you, so you'd let me get close to you. But you were too smart. You would have seen through that. Instead, I pushed you away so you wouldn't know I worked for the Crown."

"But I worked for the Crown, as well."

"Right. They left that little tidbit out of my briefing. I guess they wanted to keep it on a need-to-know basis, and they didn't think I needed to know. I'm rather peeved about that. We could have worked so well together, instead of being at odds. Then there was the Captain. He always seemed to get in my way."

"We planned to get married when the war ended."

"Figures. However, he's still living and you're not." He reached out and touched her. "I'm here for you now."

She could feel his touch and found it confusing. "Downstairs, a waiter bumped into me, but I neither upset him nor the full tray he carried. He couldn't feel me. But I can feel you. How can that be?"

"Because we're both made of the same type of spiritual energy. You have to be dead to feel it. So we can feel each other, but the living can't feel us. Nor can we feel them."

"And you know this because…?"

"It's a *Collective* thing."

"Then why don't I know it?"

"Give it time, Evie. I know you'll catch on."

She was about to speak, but stopped when she heard a key in the door lock.

"We don't have to be quiet," Nigel told her. "They can't see or hear us."

"I'm not so sure about that. When I was down in the ballroom, I went over to Bunny and she stopped speaking in mid-sentence when I got close to her, like she knew someone was there."

"Interesting."

They watched as the door slowly opened.

Evangeline raised an eyebrow and looked at Nigel, but he just stared out into the hallway. Bunny Stanton and Hutchinson Smythe were locked in an extremely passionate kiss.

CHAPTER FIVE

"Please, Antonia, come inside." Hutch led Bunny into his suite.

Bunny smiled when she spotted the luxurious trappings. Cream-colored wainscoting and crown molding accented the taupe walls. A pair of white pilasters flanked either side of the marble-clad fireplace. And the windows were dressed with sheer white curtains framed by taupe and cream silk drapes.

She ran her hand over the plush upholstered furniture and noted the rich wood furnishings. The bookcase niche overflowed with classic first editions, the silk carpet suggested unparalleled luxury, and an armload of fresh flowers sat on a credenza that housed a radio.

Hutch wrapped his arms around her. "Does my meager room meet with your approval?"

Bunny sighed. "I guess I'll just have to make

do." She allowed her stole to drop to the floor as Hutch engaged her in another passionate embrace.

Nigel pulled Evangeline closer. "Did he just call her Antonia?"

"Yes," Evangeline answered, "but I'm sure it's Bunny."

"Humph. Bunny wasn't even Bunny, or at least that wasn't her real name. It was Agatha Strang. And," he continued, "this woman has dark hair."

"I'd have dark hair, too, if Interpol wanted me."

"So," Nigel surmised, "she obviously doesn't mind changing her name or her hair color at the drop of a hat. This should be quite a performance."

They watched as Hutch retrieved Bunny-Agatha-Antonia's stole and draped it over the back of the couch. "Let's have some champagne," he cooed, caressing her arm.

"Do you think they have pink champagne? You know how much I love pink champagne."

Hutch looked longingly at the expensive bottle of Dom Pérignon he had waiting on ice. "Let me call the concierge and ask if they can send up a bottle of your precious pink bubbly."

"And strawberries. I love to watch them bobbing in the bubbles." She sat on the couch and struck a seductive pose while Hutch made the call.

"They'll send some up straightaway." He sat as close to Bunny as he dared. She was a provocative woman and he wanted to learn everything he could about her. "Tell me about yourself. Not about your acting successes, which I find quite astounding considering your heritage, but about young Lady Antonia Southerland growing up in the wilds of colonial India."

Bunny launched into a very colorful story about India.

Hutch hung on every word. Some of it sounded contrived and fantastical, but she told the story well, and he enjoyed listening to her voice as she wove herself into a very exotic tale.

"India?" Nigel looked at Evangeline.

"Well, my best guess is that Mr. Hutchinson Smythe has never been to India and Bunny feels safe saying she grew up there. There's a much greater chance he's been to England and has friends there who would tell him she's a figment of her own imagination. Lady Antonia Southerland—indeed!"

Nigel laughed at Evangeline's umbrage. "I can tell you for a fact—she's no lady."

Evangeline eyed him suspiciously. "You told me nothing happened between you and Bunny."

"And nothing did. But that's not saying she didn't try. It started the night of the Captain's dinner aboard the Queen Mary, when she began caressing my leg under the table. I said I wasn't feeling well and went back to my cabin just to get away from her. Then, she showed up at my door later that evening with champagne and glasses, and I had to find a way to get rid of her, again."

"I'm surprised you didn't take advantage of all she had to offer."

"All I could think of was you. Bunny paled in comparison."

Evangeline didn't know whether or not to believe him, but couldn't help smiling. "What do you think she's up to?"

"It's hard to tell. She obviously wants something from him, but we don't have enough information yet to know what that is."

"Well, I guess we could spy on them."

"We could do that."

"How long do you think it will take before she tips her hand?"

"What does it matter? We have all the time in the world."

Evangeline winced. "Why must everyone keep pointing that out to me?"

"I don't understand."

"A tall, bald man with a hooked nose told me I had 'forever' to wait in the 'line for Purgatory.'"

"That's Saint Peter. If you were on the line for Purgatory, how did you end up here?"

"I told him I had to find out who murdered me."

"And that's all it took?"

"I was strong. I was forceful. I argued my case logically and masterfully."

Nigel laughed. "I see. He sent you back so he could get some peace and quiet."

"Well, how come you were allowed to return?"

"I was strong. I was forceful. I argued my case logically and masterfully. And then I groveled."

They laughed together and it felt good, but then Nigel grew serious. "You know, this won't be as easy as you think. And our time together won't last forever."

"What do you mean?"

"The Celestial Hierarchy allowed us to return so we could bring our killers to justice and rest in peace. You've just told me who's responsible for my death, so my mission here is now half over. I just have to find a way to make Bunny pay for her sin. Once I do that, I'll be back at the Pearly Gates before you can say 'Peter was a fisherman.'

"It's not much fun being down here alone," he continued. "The only other spirits you see are people who were around at the time of your death and have died since then. Since you just got here yourself, the chances of you bumping into someone else are pretty unlikely. I'm surprised you could even find me. I died quite a while ago."

"Maybe it's because I recently thought about you."

"You did?"

"The Crown honored my brother Wills for his exemplary military career, and it made me nostalgic because I'd almost lost him when he was taken prisoner by the Nazis—all because they thought he had stolen documents which he hadn't stolen at all.

"You were a big part of my first mission to save my brother, and I wanted to visit your grave to thank you."

"The documents …"

"That stupid Swiss map and those pages of secret code—you must remember that."

"Of course I remember. I'm the one who stole them."

"You!"

"I had to. I heard the Nazis were planning to invade Switzerland, and I needed to learn more about it.

I can only assume your brother was trying to do the same thing.

"The Nazis caught him snooping, so I created a diversion to draw them away. When I rushed inside to liberate him, he was out cold. That's when I saw the map of Switzerland and other documents on the desk, so I took them. I tried to save your brother, as well, but Rudolph Hess and Siegfried Feuermacht had knocked him out and I couldn't revive him. I heard them returning and had to leave your brother there or I, too, would have been taken prisoner."

"Why didn't you ever tell me this?"

"I didn't know you were working for the Crown. I thought of you as a damsel in distress whom I was sent to protect. It was classified information, and by the time I found out we were working for the same side, it was too late. That's the day I died. Don't think I haven't thought about you day and night since then. All I can think about is what I would have done differently."

His admission piqued her curiosity. "What would you have done differently?"

"Well, first off, I would never have allowed you to become acquainted with the Captain."

"Jealous?"

"I'm being practical. If we had avoided the Captain's dinner, I wouldn't have been introduced to Bunny. You wouldn't have had the Captain to rely on, so you would have relied more on me, and I would have been able to protect you better." He paused. "And maybe, I was a tiny bit jealous." A look of horror crossed his face. "Don't tell me you were shot while visiting my gravesite."

"No. It happened the next day. I went straight

from the cemetery to Nuremberg, where I was scheduled to testify against a man named Heinz Bruchman. I was shot before I even walked into the building." She heard a moan coming from the other side of the room. "What are Bunny and Hutch up to?"

Nigel put his hand on her cheek to prevent her from turning around. "Let's just say they're engaged in something that's definitely not proper for a lady to see."

"I'm a big girl," she said as she struggled to turn her head. "I've been married and I certainly know what consenting adults do for … entertainment."

So did Nigel, and he did the only thing he could think of to stop Evangeline from spying on Bunny and Hutch.

CHAPTER SIX

HARRY S. TRUMAN STILL COULDN'T BELIEVE HE WON THE election for President of the United States, and he was amazed by how much more complex the job was than he had initially believed. Thank goodness he had Bess at his side to support him through the rough patches.

He had been blindsided by the Manhattan Project, but had still chosen to use atomic power to force the Japanese to surrender the war in the Pacific. Deep down he felt he'd made the right decision, and would do it again if he had to, but he had detractors who said the U.S. would still have been victorious without resorting to A-bombs.

At least today's task would be relatively simple. The United Nations General Assembly was being held in Flushing Meadows, New York, for the first time, and he would be addressing the assembly that afternoon.

He planned to go to the theater with Bess the following evening to see a musical called *Annie Get Your Gun*, based loosely on the high jinks of sharpshooter Annie Oakley.

His aide arrived to tell him it was time to leave for the UN. The drive from Manhattan to Flushing Meadows would take some time, even though the recently built Queens-Midtown Tunnel would make the trip more direct.

The United Nations had moved into some of the buildings remaining from the 1939 World's Fair. The General Assembly hall featured an impressive world map flanking a high dais, in front of a raised podium. The delegates' area contained headphones so speeches in various languages could be interpreted for them, and the massive hall had a clean, modern feel.

Truman liked what he saw, even though he knew it was only temporary. He looked forward to addressing the assembly of delegates from around the world, and hoped they would embrace America's postwar agenda.

Nigel kissed Evangeline and they kindled quite a spark.

Evangeline reluctantly pulled away. "I guess *everything* doesn't die when you're dead."

"People may die, but their energy lives on. And if they, perchance, return to the physical world, some of that energy finds their trace signature and reunites with it. That energy is what causes ghosts to generate plasma.

"Individually and under normal circumstances," Nigel went on, "the energy is not seen or felt by anyone. But when spirits become highly agitated or aroused, we generate a bit of a charge. And if two of us, together, become aroused, the sparks can fly."

"So you think I'm aroused, do you?"

Nigel smiled. "Well, let's just say I can't make my toes curl like they just did without your involvement."

"That's a very nice theory, Nigel. Now, I need another one that might help me find my killer."

Playtime had ended.

Nigel rose to the task. "Let's start with the facts and work backwards."

"All right. Fact number one: I was shot in the head."

"What did the wound look like?"

"Look, I'll show you." Evangeline pulled back her hair, exposing her temple.

"There's nothing there, Evie. You don't have your bullet wound, just like I'm here all in one piece. We no longer bear the evidence of what killed us."

"I just saw it for a moment and didn't really take the time to study it. I only remember that it was a clean shot."

"Did you see any residue?"

She tried to recall the image she had seen in the mirror.

"No, I don't think so."

"Then we can rule out anyone who was with you. Who *was* with you?"

"Only an MI6 security officer and a councilor."

"All right. Who knew you planned to be at the location where the shooting took place?"

"The Prime Minister. My brother. Everyone knew about the trials. It was in all the newspapers and was constantly talked about on the radio."

"You've got to help me out here, Evie. You're not giving me anything I can sink my teeth into."

"What if I wasn't the intended victim?"

"People just don't go around shooting other people with high-powered rifles. I think someone must have been tailing you."

"You know, I tried to go off the radar for a while after the war ended, but MI6 told me without my deposition, Heinz Bruchman might go free."

"MI6? Is it possible someone from the foreign office wanted you dead?" After thinking about it for a moment, he shook his head. "It's more likely an assassin staked out headquarters. Tell me more about Bruchman."

"He's a Nazi who stumbled upon General George Patton in France—at a time when Patton was reported to be in England getting ready to launch a secondary invasion against the Germans. Apparently, the Germans withheld troops so they could fight the incursion. If word had leaked out that Patton was already on the continent and there would be no secondary invasion, the Germans would probably have used those extra troops to prevent the Allies from pushing into Brittany—a strategy that turned the war around.

"Christian Butler and I caught up with Bruchman, just before he was scheduled to meet with the German high command. We detained him, giving the Allies an opportunity to put *Operation Cobra* into action."

"I remember Butler. I went through RAF training with him. He was MI6's number-one man. I've often wondered what happened to him."

"He was killed on the *HMS Formidable* when the plane he was readying for takeoff was hit by a Japanese kamikaze pilot."

"I'm not familiar with kamikaze pilots. What are they?"

"Suicide pilots who crash their planes into aircraft carriers and other warships to take them out of commission."

"That's crazy."

"The American ships suffered the most damage from them. Our ships were better built. Still, that didn't help Christian. His plane was fully fueled and he burned to death when the tank exploded."

"What a horrible way to die."

"More horrible than being blown apart by a grenade?"

"I didn't know what hit me. Burning to death seems a lot more agonizing."

"Could we not talk about it?" Evangeline trembled. Her demeanor had dramatically changed.

"If I didn't know you were going to marry the Captain, I would think you were sweet on Christian."

"Colin proposed to me after Christian's death. I accepted."

"Trying to fill a void?" Nigel studied Evangeline's face.

"We've gotten off topic. I was talking about my deposition against Heinz Bruchman."

"Right. About whether you had been followed."

"I could have been. I had a lot on my mind and wasn't really paying attention."

"Think. The war is over. Many of the Nazi leaders are either dead or imprisoned. Who would still be around, who wanted to stop you from testifying against

Bruchman?"

"A lover? A brother? His mother?"

"Only if Mother Bruchman is a sharpshooter with a high-powered rifle."

The thought of an elderly woman toting a military firearm made Evangeline laugh. Bruchman was in his fifties, and his mother was probably close to eighty. "I'd better check with the War Secretary to see if he had a brother."

"You can't, Evie, you're dead."

"Then how are we going to find out?"

"We need to connect with someone in the *Collective* who may have known Bruchman."

"How do we do that?"

"We just do it." Nigel took a deep breath, and disappeared.

Bunny Stanton awakened the next morning in the arms of Hutchinson Smythe. She slipped out of bed and tiptoed to the silver tray of strawberries leftover from from the night before. Popping a berry into her mouth, she headed to the bathroom to freshen up.

The bathroom in the Presidential Suite made her feel special. It had a large marble sink, with an ornate gold mirror above it. She wished the bathroom in her flat looked this good. If only she could figure out how to smuggle the beautiful mirror out of the hotel.

The one thing she didn't like about the mirror was her reflection. She felt sure the strawberries had caused her blotchy skin. She also had dark circles under her eyes, partly because she had fallen asleep with her makeup on. Thank God she had time to repair the damage before

Hutch woke up. She had nearly finished when he knocked on the door.

"Yes?" she said seductively as she peeked her head out at him. "What can I do for you this morning?"

"Nothing, darling," he said, giving her a quick kiss. "I've got to go see someone at the United Nations."

He had Bunny's immediate attention. "Take me with you. I've never been to the United Nations and would love to see it." She closed in on Hutch and nibbled on his ear. "I would be *very* grateful," she teased.

"Let me think about it while I shower. I can't take you into the meeting with me, but I suppose someone could take you on a tour of the building. It's out on Long Island, though, and you'd certainly need a change of clothing." He paused for a moment. "I don't think there's enough time for you to run home and change, darling. I'll take you with me next time."

Hutch pushed Bunny out of the bathroom and turned on the shower taps. Soon, she heard his slightly muffled baritone voice singing "I Get a Kick out of You."

Bunny refused to accept defeat. She pulled on her clothing from the night before and left him a note saying she would be right back. She took the elevator down to the lobby and visited a dress shop located inside the hotel.

The offerings were more conservative than her usual style, but they would allow her to blend in at the United Nations. She paired a white silk blouse with a navy-blue pencil skirt and cardigan, and added blue-and-white spectator pumps and a plain navy clutch. She paid for her purchase with cash she had liberated from Hutch's wallet.

She rushed back upstairs and knocked on the

door of the suite, just as Hutch was walking out of the bedroom.

He did a double take when he answered the door. "How did you manage to change clothes so quickly?"

"When I want to spend the day with an attractive man, I don't let anything get in my way." She stashed the bag with her evening clothes on the couch.

He took her arm in his and led her back outside. "I love a woman who knows what she wants," he said as he pulled the door closed behind them.

CHAPTER SEVEN

"SHE HAS TO LEARN TO CRAWL BEFORE SHE CAN WALK. You should know that better than anyone." Saint Peter vigorously rubbed his bare head with both hands while he thought about Evangeline's dilemma.

Nigel had become part of the *Collective* in 1936. Over the past decade, he had developed abilities that Evangeline did not yet possess. Saint Peter didn't want to have her running amok throughout the universe, creating problems she wasn't yet capable of handling.

He finally relented. "Look, I'll make a deal with you. I'll give you some of the information you seek …"

A gentle rumble of thunder stilled everyone around them.

"… a modicum of the information you seek. But you must not let Evangeline do anything before her time. If you're not sure, ask the *Collective*. Your best bet is to pretend you don't know how to do anything supernatural, that way she won't be tempted to seduce it out of you."

"Ouch."

"What do you think, we're blind up here? We saw the spark the two of you made. Still, a man with your MI6 experience should be able to handle her quite easily."

"Yes, sir."

Nigel reappeared at the Waldorf Astoria just as Bunny and Hutch were leaving.

"Good. You're just in time." Evangeline headed toward the door, but noticed Nigel wasn't accompanying her. "What are you waiting for? We need to follow them."

"How do you plan to do that?"

"We'll just … tail them."

"Have you ever been to the United Nations?"

Evangeline hesitated. "Yes," she said defiantly. "When they proposed the charter."

"Great. You can go to San Francisco, where they proposed the charter, while Bunny and Hutch go to Flushing Meadows."

"What do you mean?"

"The United Nations has moved since your visit there."

"Where's Flushing Meadows?"

"It's on Long Island. It's a temporary location until a permanent home is decided upon. I'm willing to bet you've never been there, since today is the first time ever that a General Assembly meeting is being held there."

"And your point is …?"

"Evie, darling, you're trying to go somewhere you haven't been before. We're each composed of a unique energy charge that leaves a trace signature wherever it's been. When we die, our energy is transmuted into a higher, psychic form that travels along the trails made during our past lives."

"And you know this because …?"

"The *Collective* thing."

"Well, I'm not receiving signals from the *Collective* thing, so excuse me if I go to the UN without you."

"We'll see. Anyway, be careful."

"This is not the time to be careful." Evangeline wanted to physically push Nigel into action. "Besides, if we put our heads together, we might find a way to travel where we've never been before, even if there are some risks involved."

"I only take calculated risks, Evie. If it doesn't add up in my favor before I make my first move, I won't act on it."

"Why are you saying this? I know you've taken risks in the past."

"Not always. If you dared me to bet a large amount of cash in a casino because I could win a bankroll, I might do it. But if you asked me take a risk in which an innocent person might get hurt, I'd have to say, 'No thank you.'"

"But you're an agent for the Crown!"

"Was."

"Excuse me?"

"We're dead, Evie. We may still try to act like spies, but we're really just disembodied spirits floating around in the ether. And if we're able to do some good, that's great. But if we can't, no one would hold it against us."

"I used to think you were dashing—even when I

thought you might be responsible for kidnapping me. I hated you, but held you in awe at the same time."

"And now?" he asked.

"Now, I think you've become a big fuddy-duddy."

"A what?"

"A really old-fashioned stick- in-the-mud. A total fussbudget. "

"Clichés? Is that all you've got to hurl at me?"

"Give me a minute." She hated his smug grin, but saw his eyes flicker as he became serious.

"You know, Evie, when I first joined the Royal Air Force, I became fast friends with a chap named Roxy. His given name was Alfred Winston Roxborough III, but that seemed too stuffy for a hotshot future wing commander, so I started calling him Roxy. And the name stuck.

"Those first few months we were inseparable. We relied on each other to calculate fuel burn and get through navigation lessons, and some of our mates used to joke that we were connected at the hip, which may not have been so bad considering some of the beauties Roxy dated. I would have gladly seconded him for any of those interludes."

"And this is pertinent to our conversation because…?"

"I'm trying to explain to you why I only take calculated risks."

"Can't you just tell me outright?"

"I'm getting to it. I never realized how impatient you are. I always thought of you as a lady who was as serene as she was beautiful. But now I see you're more like a hotheaded, petulant child."

"Criticizing me won't get us any closer to discovering what's going on here."

"I'm not criticizing you. I'm teasing you. You've even lost your ability to have fun."

"I'm sorry, Nigel." She batted her lashes at him. "Now, what were you saying about Roxy?"

"When we were taught how to parachute out of a disabled aircraft, Roxy and I differed on how we should prepare our chutes. He believed in having his packed and ready well before flight time. But I liked packing my chute at the last minute, so I could be sure there were no little surprises I might have forgotten about.

"We were tested one day with an unexpected early-morning training drill. I scrambled to pack my chute, while Roxy made fun of me. But he had forgotten that his chute had a frayed cord that needed to be replaced. If he had packed it that morning, he would have seen the problem and either gotten his hands on a different chute or missed the takeoff while trying to find one.

"Instead, he sauntered toward the plane while I rushed around like a madman."

"I jumped out of a plane and my chute wasn't packed in anything."

"That's because you probably used a static line. I'll bet it was attached to the plane and opened immediately."

"Yes."

"Our chutes were different. Our planes were too small for static lines, so we folded our chutes into something akin to a knapsack and deployed them by pulling a cord. Except when Roxy pulled his cord, it ripped off and his chute didn't open."

"How awful."

"I saw him free-fall, and there was nothing I could

do to help him because my chute had already opened.

"When I reached the ground, I ran over to him. I saw his chest heave as he gasped for air, and I knew he was in a bad way. His leg was bent in an unnatural position and there was blood trickling from his nose and mouth.

"It was a tough lesson for a young upstart like me. I came to grips with my own mortality that day, when my best friend died in my arms. We weren't even on a mission. It was just a training exercise.

"His death changed everything. I learned to be more cautious, without being so fastidious that it could come back to haunt me. And I learned to *not* take risks until I had calculated all the possible outcomes in my head. I'm good at that. I was the chess champion at Eton for two years running, and the ability to look ahead has always stayed with me."

"Except for the day you volunteered to stop at this hotel room in my place and got blown to kingdom come," she said quietly.

Nigel sighed. "Why do the people we love the most always seem to play a part in life's most painful moments?"

"I don't know how to answer that."

"It was rhetorical."

"Cut to the chase, Nigel."

"I already did. We don't make a move until we weigh the consequences and determine it's the best course of action."

"Hmm, I'm seeing you in a whole new light."

"I hope it's soft and wickedly sexy."

"Dim is a better description."

"That's so cruel."

"Love hurts," she replied as she kissed him on the cheek, and then slapped his face. "And with or without you, I'm going to the United Nations."

"Have a good time."

He infuriated her, but not enough to make her change her mind. Evangeline willed herself to appear at the United Nations. Everything momentarily went dark. When she could see again, she was in a large empty room. It looked similar to the assembly hall she had visited before she died, but appeared to have been stripped of its former identity.

She left the hall, and then the building, and found herself in a plaza overlooking the city of San Francisco. She sighed. Nigel had been right. She started walking around the city, but found she couldn't turn down certain streets that she wanted to explore.

She hopped onto a cable car, but was disconcerted when a man sat down on top of her, literally sharing her space.

She walked down to Fisherman's Wharf and looked out over the harbor at the Golden Gate Bridge. There was activity going on all around her, but Evangeline soon realized the solitude she enjoyed while alive had turned into a melancholy loneliness in death, and she desperately missed Nigel's company.

She closed her eyes and envisioned herself back at the Presidential Suite in the Waldorf Astoria.

Evangeline had been gone for hours and Nigel wondered if she would ever return. He was lounging on the sofa when she reappeared.

"I didn't think you'd be back so soon," he lied nonchalantly.

"Even though you already knew I couldn't go to the United Nations?" she replied.

"Well, I didn't want to count you out completely. If anyone could find a way to defy spiritual phenomenon, it would be you. But I guess it's not to be."

"Bunny was so determined to go to the UN, she must have an ulterior motive. I want to know what she's up to."

"Evie," Nigel said gently, "you're not here to thwart some plan of Bunny's. You're here to put your soul to rest. That's the only thing we should be concentrating on. You need to find *your* killer. And I need to bring mine to justice."

"But Bunny *is* your killer. And we've got to stop her if she's up to no good."

"Maybe the reason why we're here together is because Bunny is an important part of the puzzle. Do you think she caused your death as well?"

"I don't know."

"Well, we could go chasing after Bunny right now, but if we do manage to make her pay for my death, my time here will end. You'll have to find *your* killer all by yourself."

"I hadn't thought of that."

"If we pool our resources to find your murderer first," he continued, "then we'll be together longer and can help each other until we're both nearly at the conclusion of our missions.

"I don't want to lose you, Evie. Not now. Not ever. So let's make our time here last."

"We can do that?"

"Not indefinitely, but at least for a little while. Don't get me wrong. We'll do what we're here to do. We'll just do it very slowly. And we may have a place to start."

"Which is?"

"Bruchman is an orphan. However, he apparently had a lover who worked in the Reichstag."

"How do you … No, don't tell me. It's the *Collective* thing, isn't it?"

Nigel shrugged and grinned.

"So now what should we do?"

He pulled her close. His toes needed curling.

EG

CHAPTER EIGHT

Bunny and Hutch walked across an outdoor plaza bordered on each side by towering white flagpoles. Various international flags identifying each new member of the United Nations flapped in the breeze. Bunny eyed the temporary UN headquarters as they approached. The building was not as grand as she thought it might be, but she wasn't there for the architecture.

Inside, a uniformed guide led them to the UN Security Council, where Hutch was scheduled to testify about the conditions at his family's diamond mines in South Africa. The guard stopped Bunny as she tried to walk into the meeting room. "Sorry, miss, but visitors are not allowed here."

Bunny turned haughty. "I'm with Mister. Hutchinson. Smythe." She drew out each word, and her staccato delivery gave import to Hutch's name.

"What is your name, miss?"

"I'm Lady. Antonia. Southerland." Bunny purposely tried to sound like an indignant British peer whose presence at the UN should go without question.

"I'm sorry, your Ladyship, but Mr. Smythe has been invited to testify, and you have not." He turned to Hutch. "You go ahead, sir." He turned to Bunny. "Lady Southerland, if you'll come with me, I'll take you to the visitors' gallery."

"I need to stay with Hutchinson." She dismissed him with a wave of her hand. "I'm a visitor to your country, and having traveled to the UN with Mr. Smythe, I wouldn't want to get separated from him and not be able to find my way back to our hotel." Her voice took on the conviction of steel. "I'm sure you wouldn't want to place your job in jeopardy, if that were to occur and it was your fault."

A senior official intervened, addressing the guide. "Is everything all right, Mr. Adams?"

The guide reddened. "This is Lady Antonia Southerland, sir. Her name isn't on the guest list and I told her I'd take her to the visitors' gallery, but she insists on staying with Mr. Smythe. She says she's afraid they'll lose each other."

"Well, we couldn't have that happen, could we?" The senior official took Bunny's arm and she smiled warmly at him. "I'll take Lady Southerland to my office, where she can relax in the waiting room until Mr. Smythe is done testifying.

"Mr. Adams, stay with Mr. Smythe and bring him to my office when he's done." He turned his attention to Bunny. "That way, Lady Southerland won't get lost."

Bunny struggled to mask her fury. "I am not a young child. I do not need to be minded. I just want to stay with my escort."

The senior official tightened his grip on Bunny's arm. "I'm sorry, Lady Antonia, but this is the only way we can ensure that you'll leave the UN with Mr. Smythe."

Bunny bristled at the implied threat in the senior official's words. But Hutch either didn't pick up on it or chose to ignore it, because he merely nodded and walked into the Security Council chamber, leaving Bunny behind.

The official guided Bunny to a drab wood paneled room with no windows. It was furnished with a modern green sofa and a kidney-shaped coffee table. A reception desk, manned by an eagle-eyed woman wearing a uniform similar to the one worn by the guide, faced the couch. She looked like she could single-handedly take on an army battalion, and she kept a constant eye on Bunny.

An assortment of LIFE magazines lay on the table. Bunny finished paging through them in mere minutes. She sat quietly, looking bored, but her mind raced as she devised a scheme to get away from her keeper. She finally smiled at the receptionist and politely asked, "Could you tell me where the ladies' loo is?"

"Excuse me?"

"The loo. The water closet. What do you call it here … a restroom?"

"It's down the hall. I'll show you," the receptionist said, standing up.

"Oh no, no, no, that's not necessary. I'm sure you have plenty of work to do. I'll only be a minute."

The receptionist smiled. "I do have an important

job to do."

"I thought so," Bunny said genially.

"It's taking care of you," the receptionist said, now standing within two feet of Bunny. "Right this way."

At least she was no longer cooped up in that infernal waiting room, but she still wasn't free. She entered a stall in the ladies' room, wondering how she could lose her escort. She lost her train of thought when she heard an unfamiliar voice. "Hey, Margaret, are you going to see the President when he addresses the General Assembly this afternoon?"

"I'm not sure yet." Bunny recognized the voice of the woman guarding her. "It depends on what Mr. Bradley has going on. But I'd love to see Truman, if only so I can tell my kids I saw the President. How about you? Are you going to get to see him?"

"I'm almost sure of it. Somehow, I got roped into arranging security for the President's trip to the theater tomorrow night, even though it's the Secret Service's job."

"Yeah? What's the General going to see?"

"*Annie Get Your Gun*. And let me tell you, his security detail is driving me crazy. They want me to find a blueprint of the theater, as well as any maps of subway or service tunnels that run beneath it, where someone could sneak in.

"Apparently, the President didn't tell the Secret Service he was going to the theater until they'd already left Washington. So now they're playing catch-up and I've got to do all the grunt work."

"Are there really tunnels under the theater?"

"I don't know yet, but I know there are subways nearby. I'm waiting for someone to get back from city hall with a map of all the underground systems, especially the IRT and the BMT, so the President's people can inspect them to determine if they pose a threat."

Bunny emerged from the stall. She looked at the other woman and smiled. "I couldn't help but overhear your conversation. It all sounds so exciting. What theater is the President going to?"

"The Imperial Theater on 45th Street, but forget about trying to attend tomorrow night's performance. It's sold out. I heard getting tickets for the First Family was difficult, even though he's the President of the United States," she said with a laugh.

But Bunny wasn't interested in seeing the show. She had other plans for the evening.

Hutch testified for three straight hours before the committee felt it had enough information. Afterward, the guide led him to the senior official's office, where Bunny quietly waited.

"I hope you'll forgive me," he said, taking her hand. "If I had known it would take this long, I wouldn't have brought you with me."

Bunny smiled at him. "Don't worry, darling," she said. "I had a lot to think about."

"Let's head back into Manhattan. I know a wonderful place where we can have a late lunch. It has the largest prawns you'll ever see. And then, I think a visit to Tiffany's may be in order for a little show of my appreciation to you for waiting so long."

That afternoon, Truman was well received as he took the podium and spoke of the freedoms everyone is entitled to: freedom of speech, freedom of religion, freedom from want, and freedom from fear.

He segued into nations working together to remove the fear of weapons of mass destruction.

Finally, he assured delegates that the United States would support the United Nations, with all the resources it possessed.

He felt a small measure of relief when his speech was over. The rest of his stay in New York promised to be entertaining and relaxing.

When they finally arrived back at the hotel, Bunny wrapped herself around Hutch like a second skin. She wanted to make him very happy. But even though her tongue was in his ear, her eyes were riveted on the diamond bracelet he had purchased for her that afternoon.

CHAPTER NINE

IT STARTED OUT AS A GENTLE KISS, BUT NERVE ENDINGS popped when Nigel's lips met Evangeline's, and she passionately kissed him back. The interaction took her breath away, oddly enough, considering dead people don't breathe. She eventually pushed Nigel away and studied his face. "I didn't think I'd feel anything."

"Thanks for the vote of confidence."

"That's not what I meant. It's just that being a ghost and all, I didn't expect much. But that was pretty … um … electric."

Nigel grinned.

"You were hoping that would happen, weren't you?" she continued.

"I believe I already said that if the two of us became aroused together, the sparks would fly. So I'm only a little surprised—and in a good way. And you've got to admit that we had the same current sparking between us back in '36 when we first met. It's just that back then you didn't really trust me, so you kept pushing me away instead of allowing our mutual attraction to take hold. Some people never get the chance to feel what we just felt. Let's not analyze it. Let's build on it."

"I'm engaged to Colin." She said it very quietly.

"Colin's alive, Evie. He can't see you or feel you like I can. And unless he dies a violent death that somehow ties into ours, you may never see him again."

Evangeline didn't know what to think. She still had all the same emotional uncertainties she'd had during her lifetime. Truth be told, when she and Nigel first met, she *had* felt attracted to him. She had also felt attracted to Colin. The fact that both men acted like rivals had dissuaded her from becoming involved with either of them.

But then Nigel died, and Colin proved his mettle when he helped her rescue her brother from the Nazis. They drifted apart after Evangeline returned to New York to smoke out German spies who had landed on Eastern Long Island. During that mission her new partner, Christian Butler, literally swept her off her feet. However, Colin reentered her life after Christian died.

Now, she felt like a traitor, even though she knew Nigel was right. Colin still lived in the physical world. He might be mourning her death, but in time he would probably fall in love with another woman, maybe several of them. Or he might settle down and have a family. Suddenly, she didn't like where this particular line of thought had taken her.

"Nigel, let's do something. Let's get out of here.

There must be other places where we can go to hunt for clues."

"I was just thinking the same thing and I know a great place. But I don't know if you've ever been there. It's called the Cotton Club."

"You think we'll find clues at a nightclub?"

"It will help us relax and clear our minds."

"I've never been there. However, I have spent a few pleasurable evenings at the Copacabana."

"But I haven't. What other New York nightclubs have you gone to?"

"Just the one where that man Walter Winchell butts into everyone's business."

"The Stork Club? Terrific. Let's go." He took her hand, and a moment later they stood at the edge of the dance floor. They watched a couple of busboys put away glasses under the bar, then entered another room where workers placed crisp, starched cloths on each of the tables before setting them with china and silverware.

"I think we may have jumped the gun," she sighed. "We're too early."

"Yeah. Too bad I haven't figured out how to go forward yet. Just back."

"What do you mean?"

"Back in time. I can revisit the past, but I can't go forward into the future. I know that it's possible, but the *Collective* doesn't want me to know how to do that yet." He immediately knew he'd said too much.

A rumble of thunder rattled the glassware. The workers jumped. One of them ran over to a window and looked out. The sun blazed overhead.

Evangeline would not allow herself to be

deterred. "Are you saying we can revisit our past lives?" The prospect intrigued her.

"You don't want to do that, Evie. It sounds like it would be wonderful, but it leaves you with an extreme sense of melancholy. If you go back, you'll feel the pain of what you've lost so acutely, you'll hate *me* for taking you there."

"Please, Nigel. I just want to see Wills and his family one more time."

"I'm surprised you're not asking to visit Colin."

"Can you take me to Wills?"

Nigel hesitated. Finally, he took her hand, and a moment later they were outside the barn on the estate where Evangeline had grown up. She gave Nigel a tour of the grounds, recounting each detail of the property and pointing out every single spot where something had happened to either her or Wills as a child.

After touring the outer buildings they visited the main house, but no one was inside. They'd gone back in time exactly one week. It was Wednesday. Her brother had probably gone into town for market day.

The only place left unexplored was Evangeline's favorite part of the manor—the creamery. She took Nigel's hand and led him inside. Squeals of delight drifted down from the hayloft, and in an instant she and Nigel transported there, where they spied on her niece and nephew as they played. She watched Emma dart behind a bale of hay and Edward chase her, but the boy tripped on a pitchfork and went down hard.

Evangeline rushed over to him, and attempted to stroke his face. But in that instant Edward burst into tears, his hand covering his cheek. He went running from the creamery. Emma screamed and went running after him.

"What happened?" Evangeline looked at Nigel.

"We can't interact with them, Evie. When a spirit's energy combines with a mortal's, some people feel a drop in temperature. But others, especially people we're close to, may feel pain.

"And sometimes they see something, like a shadow or a wisp of light illuminating our spiritual presence. That's enough to scare the wits out of an adult. Imagine what it can do to a child."

"Do you think he saw me?"

"I don't know. He may have only felt you, but that would be enough to terrify him."

"Now what?"

"You can look. But you can't touch."

She felt the deep sadness Nigel had warned her about. "Take me away from here."

That evening, Evangeline and Nigel returned to the Stork Club. Nigel's clothing had miraculously changed from a blue serge suit to a white smoking jacket and black pants. However, Evangeline still wore the same gown she'd had on when she first appeared at the Waldorf Astoria.

She closed her eyes and imagined herself in a white Balenciaga confection that she had purchased in Paris before she died. She opened her eyes and looked down at her gown. She still wore the same dress.

"Nigel, how did you manage to change your clothing?"

"I don't know … it's a *Collective* thing."

"I'm still waiting to be accepted into your *Collective* thing. When does that happen?"

"It's not on a schedule. It just happens. You'll know when you're part of it." He put his hand on the back of her waist and led her to the dance floor. The orchestra played a waltz and Nigel took Evangeline in his arms. They all but melted into each other as they danced cheek to cheek. Some of the other couples left the dance floor, complaining about a sudden chill, but Nigel and Evangeline continued to dance as if there were no other people in the room.

The orchestra switched to a tango, and Nigel pulled Evangeline against him. They moved in unison, acting out their passion in the dramatic steps that symbolize the dance. It was a fiery number, and as it ended, Nigel ran his hands down the sides of Evangeline's torso before grabbing her derrière and pulling her brusquely toward him.

Evangeline pushed him back, with a look of astonishment on her face, and slapped him.

"What did you do that for?" he asked, rubbing his cheek. "It's part of the dance."

"It's not what your hands were doing. It's where your mind was going."

"How could you even know where my mind was going?"

"Apparently, it's being broadcast by the *Collective* thing," she said before storming away.

CHAPTER TEN

EVANGELINE TURNED AWAY FROM NIGEL JUST IN TIME to see Noel Dubois, her French connection during her Normandy mission, take a seat in the corner of the Stork Club's elegant dining room. She couldn't determine the identity of his companion, because the man faced away from her.

She thought it odd to see Noel at a New York night club. He'd often told her how much he hated to travel anywhere and he had claimed that he'd never been outside of Europe. She knew he detested trains, airplanes, and nautical vessels of all sizes, because complaining about them had become his mantra.

She moved closer to his table to listen in on his conversation. She arrived mid-sentence.

"... and I'm sure it wasn't anyone connected to the European affair.

"Interpol says, if they didn't know better, they'd think they were following a ghost, someone from Evangeline's first mission who had pulled the strings to facilitate the poisoning of the Swiss water supply. They say her death has his mark on it. But apparently that's crazy, because the man was found dead with a bullet in his brain, shortly after Operation CAPQuellwasser failed."

"CAPQuellwasser?"

Evangeline recognized Malcolm Payson's voice, even though she couldn't see his face. The private investigator had been her New York City contact on her first mission.

"Oui. *Quellwasser* is German for spring water, and the operation was a diabolical plot to get the Swiss to order special filters to protect their water supply from contamination. The filters were German-made and contained what amounted to poison pellets. Interpol intelligence indicated there were too few pellets to contaminate an entire water supply, but if they had been used in a more controlled environment, the results could have been devastating. The poison was a fairly recent discovery called nerve gas, because it disrupts the nerves in victims' organs, causing asphyxiation when their lungs stop working."

"Nice stuff. How'd the Nazi bastards stumble onto such a deadly mix?"

"It was apparently developed as a pesticide for leaf lice."

"So how is the supposed dead man connected to the nerve-gas scheme?"

"He engineered the entire CAPQuellwasser

campaign, and even though the Brits stole his original plans before the operation could be put into action, he still managed to launch the attack. Word soon got out the Germans had set it in motion, inspiring fear and loathing in neighboring European countries, so the Nazis killed him."

"If this Nazi mastermind is dead, why would Interpol say it looks like his work?"

"They found a special cuff link, given to him by the Führer, on a rooftop overlooking the plaza where Evangeline was killed."

"That's impossible." The words came from behind her. Nigel had been standing there, also eavesdropping on the conversation.

"But maybe it's not," she countered.

"You said they found his body, Evie. Interpol is pretty good at making positive identifications."

She wanted to believe Nigel, but the idea that her former nemesis Siegfried Feuermacht could be involved in her murder kept nagging at her.

"Dance with me, Evie. You need to distance yourself from what you just heard. You've got to give yourself a chance to digest the information before reaching any conclusions."

She allowed Nigel to lead her back to the dance floor. She settled into his arms and closed her eyes as they waltzed. A moment later her eyes sprang open, when she realized her partner had changed.

Evangeline took a step back from Saint Peter. "What are you doing here?"

"I'm here to check up on you. You returned to

earth to find your killer and I want a progress report."

She told him what she had overheard, then asked, "Is Siegfried Feuermacht dead or alive?"

"Do you know how many people pass by me each day, each week, each month, each year, each decade, each generation, each millennia, each—"

"You can stop now, I get the idea."

"I'll tell you what I'm going to do. Normally I only do this for people I really like. But I know you'll be a pain in the neck until you get the answer, so I'll check the archives and get back to you."

"Will that take long?"

"I'm only one man. As it is, there's bound to be a backup of souls waiting for me at the Pearly Gates. Who knows what kind of mischief they'll get into before I process them?

"I'll find that information for you, Evangeline. Eventually. But I can only work on it part-time."

"That very nice of you, considering you don't like me."

"I may have misspoken. I like you just as much as the next avenging ghost."

"Well, it's still nice of you. Thank you."

"Hey, what can I say? I'm a saint."

CHAPTER ELEVEN

BUNNY WALKED OUT OF THE BEDROOM TO FIND HUTCH had breakfast waiting. Wisps of steam rose from porcelain coffee cups. A platter of delicate pastries oozed with butter next to a bowl of strawberries nestled in a pool of cream. Bunny joked, "What, no champagne?"

Hutch smiled. He walked over to a silver ice bucket and pulled out a bottle of pink champagne. "Of course, darling. For you—the world."

Bunny hugged him. She had stumbled onto something wonderful, and if she played her cards right, she could end up with everything she had always wanted.

After breakfast, Bunny went down to speak with the concierge, while Hutch made business calls. She asked about tickets for *Annie Get Your Gun* and he told her he would make inquiries for her. "However," the concierge warned, "I heard the President is going to tonight's show, and it may be impossible to get tickets."

Bunny smiled at him. "This is the Waldorf Astoria. You're the best. If anyone in this town has the ingenuity to get tickets to a popular show, I'll bet it's you." She said it more as a challenge than a compliment, but she had heard the concierge could resist neither. Bunny hoped he would pull out all the stops to get her the tickets she needed. Not only would they be a surprise for Hutch, she would also be able to take care of a little business at the theater. Still, she needed a contingency plan, just in case.

"While I'm here, maybe you'll be able to help me with something else. I know New York has a tube system much like the one we have in London. I believe you call yours a 'subway.' Would you have a map of the different stations it travels to?"

The concierge handed her several pamphlets and Bunny found a seat in the lobby. She thoroughly studied the contents of the maps before she left the hotel and headed west along 50th street.

Evangeline made Nigel wait all night at the Stork Club, just in case Saint Peter returned with the information she wanted.

Nigel restlessly drummed his fingers. "Exactly what did he say to you?"

"I've already told you three times. He said he would look into it."

"But before, you used the words, 'part-time.'"

"Yes."

"Evangeline, part-time for a man who will be

around for *eternity* could take a millennium."

"Your point being …?"

"I don't mind spending a millennium with you. I would love for us to be together for all time. But I don't want to spend every moment of it here."

"I thought you liked the Stork Club?"

"I love the Stork Club, especially at night, when everyone's here. But right now is another story. The sun is coming up, and I'm sure our daytime hours could be much better spent."

"But what if Saint Peter can't find me?"

"Can't find you? Of course he can find you. He found you here, didn't he?"

"Maybe that was a lucky break."

"Evie, he's Saint Peter. He knows where every soul is at all times."

"He didn't know where Siegfried Feuermacht is."

"Maybe he just wants to double-check before sending you on a wild-goose chase."

"I guess you're right."

He took her hand and instantly they arrived back at the Waldorf Astoria, just in time to see Hutch leave.

"I guess we have the place all to ourselves," Nigel said, pulling her close.

"What good is that?"

"You know, Evie, for a Frenchwoman, you're sometimes a little short on passion."

"First of all, I'm British, not French. Only my husband was French. Second, I can be as passionate as the next person, when it's appropriate."

"What's more appropriate than being alone in a suite in a luxurious hotel with someone you're very, very fond of?"

"Being alone in a luxurious hotel with someone I'm fond of when I'm *not* waiting for a visit from Saint Peter." In an instant, the tall, bald man with the hooked nose appeared. "See, I told you so.

She turned to Saint Peter. "What did you find out?"

"Nothing. I told you it would take some time. Since you're pretty new to 'life ever after,' I'm sensing your idea of *time* might be somewhat skewed.

"I'm here because your unrelenting tenacity is making Nigel generate much stronger emissions than usual. That's often caused by stress, and I figure you're the one who's causing it. We don't want any mortals to notice Nigel's apparition."

"What do you mean? How can mortals see him if he's a ghost?"

"It's the ectoplasm. Usually, you don't produce enough to be visible, but when you do, sightings are rampant and it scares the wits out of most living beings. It's also causing problems within the *Collective*. So, I'm doing something I don't usually do. I'm sharing information with you. We don't like to give freshman specters too many details, because they have a tendency to abuse their powers. But I really need you to understand why you have to kick back and relax. And just so you won't think I'm picking on you, I'll look for …" He reached into his pocket and withdrew a notepad. "… Siegfried Feuermacht. But don't go getting all excited about it. Exercise a little patience.

"In earth hours, I probably won't find this Feuermacht fellow's folder for months, maybe even years. You have no idea how backed up central records are. Some Phoenicians went on a rampage recently after they found out Egypt is still prospering, while Phoenicia is not, and they ravaged all our files. But I digress."

"Just give Nigel a break and don't stress him out. We don't want any unnecessary *sightings*."

"Exactly what do you mean by '*give him a break*'?"

"I mean, give him a little cuddle here, a little nookie there. … Help him relax."

"Are you promoting promiscuity?"

"I'm not promoting anything. I'm advising you against actions that lead to excessive ectoplasmic emissions."

"How can you say that? When we kiss, there are emissions galore!"

"Yes, but that's here behind closed doors, where no one will be the wiser."

Saint Peter suddenly looked over Evangeline's shoulder and pointed. "What's that?"

EG

CHAPTER TWELVE

NEW YORK CITY SUBWAYS COEXISTED IN A STATE OF flux. The city had purchased the various privately owned rapid-transit lines that crisscrossed Manhattan and the outer boroughs and planned to unify them into one cohesive unit, but it was a slow task.

Stations still carried the names of the older lines: the Interborough Rapid Transit Company, or IRT; the Brooklyn-Manhattan Transit line, known as the BMT; and the IND, which got its name because the city built it—*independent* of the privately owned systems.

The various legacies of the different lines resulted in quirks, making a few stations unlike any others, including the IND station at Eighth Avenue and 42nd Street, which had a unique feature. This particular line had an unused lower level with a southbound track and platform that ran beneath the regularly used tracks. It was rumored, but unproven, that the deeper level had been built during the highly competitive era of autonomous subway lines, to block any expansion plans by competitors.

The IND's lower level served passengers who wanted to cross over between the uptown and downtown trains at 42nd Street. Few people, in their rush to get from one platform to another, noticed the door under the stairs at the north end of the walkway. It led to a corridor that connected the subbasements of buildings in the theater district. It had been built as a convenience for theatergoers who wanted to travel to their favorite shows without having to brave inclement weather or mingle with the pedestrian traffic on already busy sidewalks, but the idea had all but been abandoned. Still, the door remained, a relic from the past.

When Bunny reached Eighth Avenue, she followed the signs to the southbound IND train. She paid a nickel for her ticket and took the express train one stop to 42nd Street, where she lingered on the platform, studying the station and the people using it. Once the crowd dispersed, she descended the stairs to the lower level and looked for a passageway leading to nearby theaters. She easily found the door beneath the stairwell.

Bunny turned the knob, first pushing, and then pulling. *Locked.* She removed a small metal nail file from her purse and went to work. The file had a hooked end to make cleaning under fingernails easier, but it also turned out to be a dandy gadget for breaking and entering. Bunny prided herself on her ability to pick any lock in less than sixty seconds, and her talent didn't fail her.

She pulled the door open and disappeared inside a dark corridor. Removing a flashlight from the depths of her purse, she illuminated her path. The musty passageway had a poured concrete floor and concrete-block walls, and she gagged at the overwhelming odor of urine and mildew.

Overhead, Bunny could see the outlines of bulbs hanging from light fixtures, but their power had apparently been cut and they gave off neither light nor warmth.

She eventually came to heavy door with a metal plaque affixed to it: *44th Street*. Bypassing it, she walked a few hundred feet to a similar entrance for 45th Street. She picked the lock and found a staircase leading up to a corridor filled with even more doors. She trained her torch on the first one on her right. It had an engraved sign that said *Theatre Masque*, although a hastily scribbled piece of paper had been affixed right above it, with the words *John Golden Theater*. Further down, an entryway on the left identified the *Imperial Theatre*.

Bunny inserted her nail file and jiggled it around until she felt the pin. *Click.* Inside, she found steep stairs, cluttered with old props and discarded scenery. A wooden door stood partially ajar at the top of the steps. She picked her way through the debris, squeezed through the door, and found herself on the lower level of the theater. With the light from her flashlight, she could make out the trapdoors leading up to the stage. Further away, she saw an entrance to the orchestra pit.

It reminded her of her early days as an actress, but instead of a pleasant reminiscence, her soul filled with instant hatred of the person who Bunny believed had stolen her stage career, her cousin Lynn.

She abandoned her reverie when an overhead light suddenly came on.

CHAPTER THIRTEEN

"Let's discuss ectoplasm."

Nigel eyed Evangeline, warily. "What do you want to know?"

"What do you know about people being able to see you when you're stressed out?"

"Only what Saint Peter said."

"But it seems to me, it would be easy to work ourselves into a state of stress for the sole purpose of being seen."

"Why must you do that?"

"What?"

"You always have to come up with ways to *master* a situation. Why can't you just keep your ectoplasm to yourself?"

"Nigel, we may be able to use that bit of information to bring Bunny to justice. And if Feuermacht is still alive and responsible for my death, we may be able to use it against him, as well. Isn't that why we're here?"

"I thought we'd agreed to take our time, so we could be together longer?"

"You always did defend her."

"Who?"

"Bunny."

"I'm not defending her. It's just that …" Nigel stopped when a bright flash blinded him.

When he could finally see again, Saint Peter stood before them.

"Nigel, you're emitting, again."

"I can't help it," Nigel said, his voice strained. "It's her." He all but pointed toward Evangeline.

"I have no choice, then," Saint Peter said, grabbing hold of Evangeline's hand. A moment later, she found herself back at the Pearly Gates.

"No!" she pulled her hand away from Saint Peter's grip. "What are you doing? I'm not done yet."

"I can't have you down there upsetting the locals. I told you about ectoplasm emissions to get you to stop egging Nigel on. But there you go, trying to control emissions for your own purposes, and I just won't have it."

"I demand you send me back."

"Ain't gonna happen."

"I want to see your superior, right now."

"We've been through that already. You had your chance to rest in peace. You are not allowed to disturb the peace of others. Your 'Eternal Peace' privileges have been revoked for conspiracy to emit ectoplasm without due cause."

"How am I supposed to know that's illegal?"

"It's in the handbook."

"What handbook? I don't know anything about a handbook."

An angel materialized next to Saint Peter and made eye contact. The tall, bald man with the hooked nose groaned. "Please."

The angel faded from sight, but returned a moment later with a shining piece of gossamer that looked like glass cloth with writing on it. Saint Peter handed it to Evangeline. "Read this."

As she looked at the document, the words started to scroll down. It was filled with lots of *whereas*es and *therefore*s, and as she read, additional paragraphs crowded the page, until the print became so small she thought her eyes would implode.

The scroll slowed to a crawl at one particular location:

RULES AND REGULATIONS PERTAINING TO THE NEWLY-DEAD, REMANDED TO THEIR HOME WORLDS

Public ectoplasmic emissions are strictly prohibited.

WARNING: Stress resulting in excess ectoplasm should be avoided.

The scroll again picked up speed, until the words

finally stopped. "All right, I read the handbook."

"Go back to the part that says 'I do so swear' and sign it."

"How can I sign it? It isn't paper, and I don't have a pen."

"Just touch the words *I do so swear.*"

She did and her signature magically appeared on the page. Saint Peter did the same. The handbook floated off into the heavens. "Now, can I go back?"

"Yes, but if I catch you breaking one more Celestial law, you'll be spending eternity in Limbo."

A low groan coming from the heavens caused Saint Peter to cringe.

Evangeline should have signed the elementary-level contract. She erroneously received the handbook for advanced-level spirits. She should never have been allowed to see it. It contains way too much detailed information for her to have knowledge of so early in her afterlife. It's your responsibility to make sure she doesn't run amok with it.

Another low groan came directly from Saint Peter.

"You know, you're lucky," Nigel told Evangeline. "You got off on a technicality. If they had finished your processing before you came here to avenge your murder, they would have insisted that you sign the handbook on the spot. If you had, you wouldn't be here right now."

"I can't believe that man is the be-all and end-all of everything that goes on up there."

"He's Saint Peter. He's doing his job."

"Yes, but he still has to answer to someone. There

must be some kind of tribunal that addresses wrongs."

"There is, but they're tougher than he is."

"Who are they?"

"Didn't you read the handbook?"

"I scanned it very quickly. Refresh my memory. Who's in charge?"

"The Celestial Hierarchy."

"Be more specific."

"When you have a problem in life, you take it to High Court. If you don't like the verdict, you go to the Court of Appeals. And if that doesn't work out, you can take your case to the Supreme Court. It's like that with the Celestial Hierarchy. Angels are High Court. Then there are Archangels and Principalities. The Powers and the Virtues are like the Supreme Court."

"Have you ever seen a Virtue?"

"No. But I'm not disputing the *Collective*. Evie, you've got to forget everything you learned in the physical world. Embrace the *Collective*."

"Look, I read the handbook. I know the consequences. But I feel like the *Collective* is holding out on me. I never seem to be privy to the information that you have."

"Did you ever take music lessons as a child?"

"What does that have to do with anything?"

"First you learn to play scales. Then you're taught a simple song. Once you get better at reading music, you're given more complex orchestrations. It's like that with the *Collective*. You'll get what you need, when you're ready for it."

"This is so frustrating."

Nigel pulled Evangeline into an embrace, but she

pushed him away. "I'm not the bad guy, Evie. And I know you feel something for me. I just don't understand why you keep pushing me away."

"It's complicated."

"What is? Not me, that's for sure. I told you how I feel about you. What happened that makes you want to create a buffer around yourself and prevents you from getting close to someone like me, who not only loves you but is the only man who can see you?"

"Saint Peter can see me."

"So you're pushing me away so you can have an affair with Saint Peter?"

Evangeline sighed. "Let me tell you a story.

"It happened in 1921. My brother's roommate Edmund had invited him to his family's country house for Christmas and had convinced Wills to write home to say he would not be spending the holidays with our family. Both my parents wrote back in protest, but Wills insisted on going to Edmund's house, saying he was a grown man and would make his own decisions.

"Truth be told, Edmund was a very dynamic individual. He had an engaging personality and was difficult to say no to. He had befriended Wills the moment they met, and my brother was somewhat in awe of him.

"According to Wills, when Edmund walked into a room, everything livened up and the conversation level increased. He laughed and joked with ease, was self-effacing when it suited his purposes, but had a sharp wit that Wills said could cut like a sword if Edmund chose to use it—and he often did—to elicit laughs at the expense of others. He was a good-looking young man, who had lived a life of privilege. By the time he turned twenty-one, he was already a well-traveled bon vivant, who oozed self-confidence.

"Edmund had shown Wills all around the schools that make up Oxford University, and gave my brother tips on which classes to take and background on the professors teaching them. He also introduced him to the local pubs and card clubs and encouraged my brother to stay out late carousing with him, with the promise that they'd get their class work done the following morning.

"Nothing was ever a problem for Edmund, but Wills's work suffered because he didn't work as fast as his friend, and he refused to hand in ill-conceived or sloppy assignments. He told me Edmund would just laugh at him and say, 'You'll catch on, soon enough.' Wills said he often felt a bit inferior when he followed Edmund around, but somehow, he still felt honored that Edmund associated with him."

"This is a very interesting story, Evie, but what has it got to do with us?"

"Be patient, Nigel. I'm getting to that.

"Wills often wrote me letters describing their escapades. His admiration for Edmund was evident in every word, so after hearing Wills had rebuffed our parents' request to return home for the holidays, I decided to take matters into my own hands. On my way home from Les Fougères boarding school, I made a detour to Oxford to speak to Wills in person.

"I sent word that I would be waiting for him at the front gate at 8:00 p.m., but when I got there, I found Edmund waiting instead of my brother. He introduced himself to me by saying, 'Of course, you're Vix.' And I must admit, he charmed me every step of the way, explaining that Wills was being tutored and had asked Edmund to take me to dinner.

"I remember sitting in the corner of a small pub near the school, listening to Edmund talk about all the wonderful times he and my brother had together. And all the while, he gazed into my eyes with a warm smile on his face. He told me how he would have recognized me anywhere because Wills had described how beautiful I was, and he claimed Wills was right.

"I remember feeling flattered, though surprised that Wills would ever say anything like that, because it didn't seem like something he would do.

"When I asked Edmund if he had any sisters, he said 'no,' but told me I could be his 'unofficial' sister because I was related to Wills. He even invited me to his home for Christmas, saying I'd love the great feast his family prepares for the holidays.

"But that reminded me of why I was really there, and I told him honestly that I had come to convince Wills to accompany me home for Christmas.

"I remember Edmund saying that Wills had been 'all through that' already with our parents. And he sounded intractable when he announced, 'William is coming home with me.'

"I refused to believe him. I folded my napkin, placed it on the table, and told him I wanted to go see my brother. Edmund said Wills should be in his room by then, and led me back to the university dormitories, through a creaky, old gate and across a dark square to a centuries-old building. It was like walking through a maze. We went up a steep staircase, crossed a landing, and then climbed another staircase. There was hardly a sound in the building as we walked down narrow hallways and through passages that connected to other buildings. Finally, he took out a key and opened the door to a cramped room, where he turned on a lamp and lit a fire in the grate.

"I was surprised Wills wasn't there, and asked what time he would be back. But instead of giving me a straight answer, Edmund told me that Wills wasn't doing well with his coursework and said that's why he had invited him for Christmas. He was going to tutor Wills during the holiday.

"I guess that made me suspicious. Wills had never needed tutoring before. He had always been a wonderful student, and I said as much. But Edmund had the audacity to make fun of our upbringing by saying, 'Well, this isn't some country school in Yorkshire. It's Oxford.'

"I countered by saying Wills had not attended 'some country school in Yorkshire,' but had been educated at the Royal Naval Cadet Academy at Osborne before transferring to Oxford. Edmund just manipulated the conversation, throwing the blame for bad grades back on Wills.

"I was sitting in the corner of a settee that was pushed up against a wall across from the fireplace, and Edmund sat down beside me. I remember feeling uncomfortable because our bodies were touching. He asked if I'd like something to drink, saying he had some 'awfully good whisky.' He retrieved a large flask hidden behind a secret panel built into the fireplace mantel, and he quickly gulped some of the contents. He apologized for not having any glasses.

"I felt the hairs on my arms bristle. I thought he

had brought me back to Wills's room, but apparently that wasn't the case. Edmund just pretended it was a misunderstanding and claimed he had never said we were in Wills's room.

"When I told him *that's* where I had asked to be taken, the conversation degenerated into a game of words.

"I finally got up and walked to the door, but Edmund got there first and blocked the exit. When I asked him to get out of my way, he mocked me, saying I couldn't find Wills without his help because I didn't know my way around. Then, he grabbed me and kissed me. I fought him, but he swung me around and pinned me against the door. He began biting my neck, and when I screamed, he slapped me so hard that I was stunned into silence. He told me I could scream when he wanted me to scream.

"He grabbed the front of my dress and ripped it open. The buttons popped off, making tiny ticking sounds as they hit the hardwood floor. I screamed again and gouged his face with my fingernails, but he punched me and my head hit the door, nearly knocking me out.

"I felt him yanking my skirt up over my hips when someone knocked on the door. I heard my brother calling Edmund's name.

"I screamed, 'Wills,' but Edmund stuffed his fist in my mouth to prevent me from saying anything else.

"Wills wanted to know what was going on and I could hear him jiggling the doorknob, trying to force it open. We'd had a secret knock that we used as kids, and I used it to signal him. It went something like this …" Evangeline tried to demonstrate the knock, but couldn't because her hand passed right through the table.

"Well, anyway, it sounded something like knock … knock … knick-knock. Wills recognized it and screamed out my name. He demanded that Edmund open the door, and when his 'great chum' ignored him, Wills threw himself against the door. He kept doing it, trying to force the door open. I heard the wood squeal as it finally ripped away from its hinges and crashed down into the room. Unfortunately for me, I ended up beneath it.

"Wills later told me that Edmund was halfway out an open window by the time Wills got into the room. As Edmund climbed down a drainpipe, he claimed we would never be able to make anyone believe that he had done anything wrong.

"Wills didn't see me at first and he grabbed Edmund's shirt, asking him where I was. Edmund tried to wrench free of Wills's grasp, but lost hold of the drainpipe and fell to the pavement below.

"Meanwhile, I lay battered and bleeding under the splintered door."

"My God, Evie, that's terrible."

"They say when the ambulance arrived Wills was cradling me in his arms. I awoke in a hospital and felt Wills's tears washing my face. He always denies that he cried, but I know in my heart that he felt we had both been violated."

"What happened to Edmund?"

"His brain stem broke in the fall. He remained in a coma for several days until his body gave up the ghost, so to speak, and he died. I know Wills believes that if he hadn't grabbed Edmund's shirt, Edmund wouldn't have lost his grip and fallen. However, the testimony of a student who witnessed what happened, after hearing the commotion from an adjoining room, cleared Wills of any wrongdoing in Edmund's death."

"What about you, Evie? How badly were you hurt?"

"I had a broken wrist, a concussion, and facial cuts. I lost a tooth. I remember it taking weeks for Edmund's bite mark on my neck to fade away. Plus my chest, arms, and legs were all badly bruised.

"But the emotional scarring was worse. I cried for days, so upset by the attack that I didn't return to school for the remainder of the year. I had never been afraid of men before that, but Edmund changed everything."

"I'm surprised you let your guard down enough to get married, after that."

"That's because I already knew Philippe. *Our* relationship suffered, as well, but we managed to get past it because we truly loved each other.

"Anyway, it takes me a while before I can really relax with a man, especially one who's suave and handsome and smarter than he needs to be."

"Is there a compliment buried in that? Or a criticism?"

"It's a warning to stop needling me when my passion runs hot and cold."

CHAPTER FOURTEEN

Bunny slipped back behind the door to the stair-well and held her breath. She didn't think anyone saw her, but couldn't be sure. *The sooner I get out of here the better*, she thought, as she tried to work her way through a debris field of long-forgotten scenery.

"It's around here somewhere." The deep, masculine voice couldn't be more than ten feet away from her and Bunny, afraid that she might trip over something and give herself away, froze in place.

"I could swear I put them right here."

"Maybe they're in the stairwell," a raspy-voiced man replied. "I moved a lot of junk in there last week to make space for the new shipment."

Damn. She was going to have a hard time explaining what she was doing there. She saw the shaft of light shining through the partially opened door widen as a disembodied hand pulled it open.

"Found it," the guy with the raspy voice called out.

"Thank God," replied the other man. "I would hate to hear what Miss Merman had to say if you told her you lost it."

Bunny stared at the door. The hand pulled away, but the men continued to discuss scenery and props.

"These hoop skirts have got to go. They take up too much space and we could use this rack backstage."

The door pulled open and Bunny cringed. An armful of costumes came crashing down on her. She grasped the banister and held her breath, hoping the worker wouldn't spot her as he flung hoop skirts into the stairwell.

When the light finally went out, Bunny didn't stick around. She lit her flashlight and found her way out of the theater, slowly following the corridor back to the station until she resurfaced on the lower platform.

She had been handsomely paid for a big assignment and all her advance information appeared to be spot-on. Now, she only needed to execute the plan.

A new guest quietly arrived at the Waldorf Astoria hotel, where he registered as Sebastian Faust. He wore a soft felt hat, thick horn-rimmed glasses, and a plain brown suit. As long as he kept to himself and didn't ask for any assistance from the hotel employees, he was pretty sure he would remain entirely unremarkable.

A bellboy showed him to one of the more modest rooms, which suited him just fine. The less noteworthy he seemed, the less he would be noticed. The small room didn't have much light coming in the window, but it had its own bathroom and the bed looked comfortable. After tipping the bellman, he quickly unpacked. *Time for a little reconnaissance.*

He used the stairs to get down to the garage level and pretended to be waiting for a car. When he felt sure no one paid any attention to him, he slipped through a door leading to a freight elevator and made his way down to a railroad siding that lay beneath the hotel.

Track 61 had received attention from the local newspapers when Franklin Delano Roosevelt had used it to slip into the hotel unnoticed; however, its infrequent use had rendered it nearly as forgettable as Faust hoped *he* could be.

The private siding had all the makings of a myth: a special railroad platform used by rich dignitaries whose private trains could deposit them directly beneath the Waldorf Astoria, so they could check into their rooms without having to deal with the public.

The platform meant there were underground tunnels, accessible through the hotel freight elevator, that connected to other subway tunnels and would provide a covert route to places in the city, without a traveler being seen entering or leaving those locations.

He had done his homework. He wanted to leave as little to chance as possible, and he knew if he was meticulous, he could pull off a feat that would leave people scratching their heads for years to come.

When Bunny returned to the hotel, the concierge beckoned her. "Lady Southerland, I have the tickets to the show you requested."

Bunny smiled a mile wide. She reached into her bag and pulled out a fifty-dollar bill. The tickets cost only a third of that, but she insisted the concierge keep the change. "I'm sure getting these tickets required quite a bit of work on your part, and you deserve to be compensated." She folded his hand around the bill. "I'm sure Mr. Smythe will be very grateful."

Mission accomplished.

The concierge stared at Lady Southerland as she walked away. Her hair was not as neatly combed as usual, and the back of her clothing was dirty. It looked like she had leaned against a surface that hadn't been cleaned in a long time. He made a note to send up a bellman to ask if she wanted her garments laundered.

The faux Mr. Faust, as he referred to himself, had a close call in a tunnel connecting to Grand Central Station.

While Track 61 was rarely used, the other tunnels had regular service, and he came close to being hit by an oncoming train when he tried to sidestep a rat. The faux Mr. Faust survived. The rat wasn't as lucky.

Faust decided to continue his route onboard, rather than outside the trains. Destination: Times Square.

"What are you thinking about, Evie?"

"Noel Dubois said Siegfried Feuermacht could still be alive. My first question is, how could he have tricked Interpol into believing he was dead? And my second question is, if he's alive, what is he doing here in New York?"

"Aren't you forgetting the third question?"

"What's that?"

"Is he your murderer?"

"That goes without saying."

CHAPTER FIFTEEN

"Darling, I think it's wonderful that *you* want to take *me* to the theater." Hutch lifted Bunny off the floor and twirled her around before planting a huge kiss on her lips. "I love a woman who shows initiative."

Bunny beamed. She hadn't been sure how Hutch would feel about her taking him to see *Annie Get Your Gun*, but he appeared to be genuinely happy about it.

"After dinner," he continued, "I'm taking you to Sardi's. They make the best gin and tonics, although I bet you'd prefer an Alexander, which I've heard is just as wonderful."

"Whatever you want, Hutch. I'm just happy to be in your company." When it came to twisting men around her little finger, Bunny was no slouch. She had taken a calculated risk with the theater tickets, but now that it had met with his approval, she knew it wouldn't be long before she had Hutch eating out of her hand.

Evangeline and Nigel returned to the Waldorf Astoria in time to see Bunny and Hutch dressing for the theater.

"What do you think she's planning?" Evangeline asked.

"Why does she have to be planning *anything*?" Nigel countered. "Can't she just feel like going to see a show without an ulterior motive?"

"Not Bunny. Not by a long shot."

"Well, then, I guess the question is, have you ever been to the Imperial Theatre?"

"I think so. I think I saw something there several years ago. I remember someone singing 'My Heart Belongs to Daddy,' because I sang it to myself every day for a month."

"I'm not familiar with it … but … ummm … the *Collective* says it was good."

"The *Collective*. Funny how they didn't include me in that little missive."

"They say you're too much of a maverick and they're not going to treat you like part of the team until you become a team player."

"That's ridiculous. Just because I got a little mixed up about the approved uses of ectoplasm is no reason to ostracize me."

"They're waiting for you to prove yourself."

"Prove myself, how?"

"By doing something commendable."

"What if I never do something the *Collective* thinks is commendable?"

"They'll vote to remove you from earth and force you onto a different path."

"So if they don't think my intentions are honorable, I end up on the line for Limbo?"

"Not Limbo …"

"Wonderful."

While Nigel and Evangeline bickered, Bunny and Hutch finished dressing and headed for the door.

"I think we'd better go." Nigel took Evangeline's hand, and a moment later the room was empty of both the living *and* the dead.

Bunny and Hutch were among the first to arrive at the Imperial Theatre, and were led to a private box. Hutch settled in, but Bunny leaned over and whispered that she wanted to powder her nose. He opened his Playbill and told her to take her time.

She disappeared down the stairs and stopped at the coatroom to check her fur and the jacket to her dinner suit. She also stopped in the ladies' lounge, where she removed her earrings and glasses and pulled on a beret she had in her purse. Then she talked her way into the back of the theater, saying Miss Merman had a problem with her costume, and Bunny had been sent to fix it.

"Ellen's back there. Why isn't *she* fixing it?"

"Look, all I know is I was told to come here and see Miss Merman, because she likes the work I do on her personal wardrobe."

"Oh, for crying out loud, go." The man pushed Bunny through the door. "And make it quick."

Backstage buzzed with so much last-minute

activity, no one paid any attention to Bunny as she sauntered over to the props, except Evangeline.

Nigel stuck his head through the curtain to check out the audience. Behind him, Bunny switch the gun she carried in her purse with one of the guns that would be used in the show. After she deftly pulled off the swap, she disappeared out the door before anyone noticed—that is—anyone made of flesh and blood. Evangeline witnessed the exchange and yanked Nigel back so quickly, the curtain actually moved.

She stared at it for a second, mesmerized, then returned to the problem at hand. "Bunny switched the prop gun with a real one. We've got to find out what she's up to."

"What are you talking about?"

"You'll see."

The ghostly pair found Bunny in time to watch her pull off the beret, replace her earrings and glasses, and reclaim her jacket and fur.

Back at the box, Hutch looked up and smiled. "Back so soon?"

"I just couldn't stay away from you, darling."

"Nigel, we've got to do something. We have to switch the gun back." Evangeline couldn't help acting like an MI6 agent, dead *or* alive.

Nigel had had more time to adjust to the spirit world. "That's a little beyond your skill level."

"Then what's telekinesis?"

"Where did you hear about telekinesis?" he asked in amazement.

"In the *Collective Handbook*."

"I'm surprised they showed you that, considering your recent history."

"Why does this conversation have to include my recent history?"

"Because telekinesis is the ability to move matter with your mind, and there are regulations against it."

"Why?"

"For the most part, when we touch something in the corporeal world, our hand goes right through it. We can't feel it. It doesn't move for us. We move through walls and doors, and time for that matter ... uh ... forget I said that. Anyway, we must follow a path we've traveled in life. We're specters that nobody sees. At least, we're *supposed* to remain unnoticed. That's the way it's meant to be.

"Except, there are certain instances when we *are* visible and the Celestial Hierarchy has banned us from knowingly engaging in any activity that may allow living beings to see us or sense our presence. That would include leaving an ectoplasm trail or moving objects in defiance of known physical laws."

"But, if we put our minds to it, we can move objects?"

"Sorry, Evie, this discussion is over."

"Good God, Nigel, when did you become such a ineffectual intellectual? You used to be one of the bravest, most daring wing commanders working for MI6. Nothing scared you. Now, you won't even enter into a discussion with me."

"I used to be a member of the Royal Air Force, where I learned discipline and chain of command, and I know how to work within given parameters."

"All I'm asking is if it's something you've actually seen done. Have you ever seen a ghost, like us, move something with his mind?"

"Yes."

"From one place to another?"

"Yes."

"And it worked?"

"Yes."

"I have to know, Nigel. Was it you?"

CHAPTER SIXTEEN

Nigel thought long and hard about Evangeline's question and chose his words carefully. "Evie—"

She cut him off before he even got started. "Bunny switched the gun, Nigel. Someone is going to be shot. If you know telekinesis, I suggest you use it now."

"To do what, Evie? If she took the gun with her, I can't get it back. It's buried in her handbag."

"That gun is probably harmless. It's a prop. But the gun she replaced it with may be loaded. Someone could get hurt."

"So what would you like me to do?"

"Just make the one in the prop box disappear."

"I'm not a magician. I can't make things vanish."

"That's not what I mean. When no one's looking, move the gun in the prop box to some out-of-the-way place where it won't be found in time for the show. They'll have to come up with an alternative plan because they won't be able to use Bunny's gun."

A group of chorus girls started lining up in the wings. They wore white buckskin skirts and red-and-white plaid shirts decorated with red fringe. Cowboy hats and short white leather boots completed their outfits. And each girl wore a leather holster sporting a shiny silver gun around her hips. Their black fishnet stockings seem incongruous, but after all, this *was* Broadway.

"Look all around you, Nigel. There are plenty of guns they can use. We just don't want them to use the one Bunny planted in the prop box."

"I'm going to end up in hell for this." He paused for a moment and then sighed. "Show me where the gun is."

As the overture began to play, Bunny took Hutch's arm. "I'm so excited. I've heard a lot about this show. I just know it's going to be a blast."

"My goodness, Antonia, you sound so … American. I would have expected you to say you heard the show was 'smashing' rather than 'a blast.' I hope you're not using Americanisms for my benefit. I love every little British thing about you."

Bunny sighed contentedly. He had practically said he loved her, even though he didn't use those three little words directly. "Darling, if it's British you want, it's British you'll get. I won't use another American saying, ever."

"Here, I brought these along for you." He handed Bunny a gold lorgnette. "I wouldn't want you to miss anything."

"Hutch, that's so sweet. I'll cherish this as much as I cherish the bracelet from Tiffany's."

"Sorry, darling, I can only lend this to you. It's been in my family forever, and it's one of my mother's precious heirlooms. I just happened to have it in my jacket pocket because I was carrying it for her last week when we saw *Faust* at the Met."

"Oh." Bunny's disappointment was palpable.

"If it will make you feel better, I'll get you one of your own." He kissed her cheek.

The overture seemed to be unending, and just as Hutch opened his mouth to comment on it, he was distracted by some activity in a private box directly across from them. Hutch grabbed the lorgnette and peered through it. "It's the President," he said in amazement.

Bunny feigned ignorance. "Really? Here at the same show that we're at? Well, now I can say with certainty that this will be an evening we'll never forget."

Evangeline showed Nigel the gun.

He sighed before taking her arm and tugging her back into the shadows.

"What are you doing? No one can see us."

"Maybe not now, but they'll be able to see *me* if I try to move the gun while standing right in front of the prop box. I already know there will be emissions."

"You've got to do it, Nigel. If you get caught, I'll tell Saint Peter it was my fault."

Nigel laughed involuntarily. No one would have to tell Saint Peter what happened. He would just know.

Nigel grew still while he concentrated on the gun. His brain waves sprang into action. He willed the gun to rise out of the box, and levitate toward where they were standing—very slowly. It took all of Nigel's concentration just to hold the gun in the air. Evangeline wanted to rush him, but knew it would be futile. She just prayed no one would see the gun or Nigel's emanations. Just as the gun reached a corner of the stage near the curtain, the stage manager pushed through the chorus girls, and headed straight for the ghostly duo. His sudden appearance broke Nigel's concentration and the gun dropped to the floor.

CHAPTER SEVENTEEN

A SQUEAL FROM A CHORINE WHO HAD JUST SPOTTED President Truman diverted everyone's attention and no one noticed the gun hitting the floor. However, Nigel's stress level had reached the point where it made him partially visible. Another impressionable chorus girl wiggled her way out of the group of performers who had crowded together to get a glimpse of the President, and she turned in time to see Nigel's glowing outline. Her eyes opened as wide as her mouth, but if she wanted to scream her vocal chords betrayed her, because nothing of volume passed her lips, which quivered in the shape of a perfect O.

"Damn!" Nigel couldn't help himself.

Evangeline grabbed him and pulled him behind a backdrop. She rubbed his back gently, telling him everything would be all right if he would just calm down and disappear. It took a while for his emanations to fade.

"What's with you, Millie? You look like a guppy, with your mouth opening and closing like that. You know, like a fish?" The girl who said it mimicked a guppy, and everyone within viewing distance laughed.

Millie hardly noticed her. She was too busy trying to process what she had just seen.

"Hey, kid, are you all right?" The stage manager touched Millie lightly on the arm.

The young dancer finally found her voice, or at least part of it. "Gh-gh-gh-ghost," she stammered, pointing to where she had seen Nigel.

"Was he really ugly, with bulging eyes and a noose around his neck?" Jimmy, one of the chorus boys, teased. He was good-looking, talented, and he liked girls.

Millie had a huge crush on him. She felt herself blush. She could take that kind of razzing from anyone else and dish as good as she got. But because Jimmy said it, her face reddened and she refused to say another word about seeing a ghost. Instead, she dredged up some forced bravado as she took her place in line. "Isn't this show ever going to begin? I've got a date later, and I don't want to keep him waiting."

She didn't really have a date, but Jimmy didn't know that, and it wouldn't hurt to make him think she was in demand. At least, that's what she hoped. Luckily, the music saved her from having to say another word.

The overture ended. The ensemble tapped their way onto the stage, and when Ethel Merman sang "There's No Business Like Show Business," everyone who witnessed Millie's fright immediately forgot about it.

Except Millie.

"That was close."

"I'm sorry, Nigel." Evangeline continued to soothe him. "But you did the right thing. Who knows what might happen if you didn't move the gun?"

"I guess that means you want to wait here to see what happens when someone realizes it's missing?"

"That's exactly what I plan to do."

"Great." Nigel closed his eyes as he hovered by a large sandbag. "Let me know when it's time to go."

"That's it? You're not interested in the gun?"

Nigel moved closer to the wall. "Emanations are exhausting, Evie. I couldn't be more tired if I swam across the English Channel. Let me know what you find out."

Evangeline watched as scene after scene played out on the stage. The show was extremely entertaining, and every song by Ethel Merman reverberated throughout the theater, inciting thunderous applause from the audience. Toward the end of the second act, Evangeline heard the actress complain to the stage manager that she couldn't find her gun in the prop box.

"Calm down, Ethel," he replied. "We'll get you another gun."

"Yeah, but that gun matches the one I'm already wearing. And they were specially balanced for me so I could twirl them. I hope a different gun doesn't louse up the act."

He handed her another gun. "You'll make it work, Ethel. You're a pro."

Evangeline woke Nigel. "If something is going to

happen, it's going to happen now."

Ethel Merman had no choice but to return to the stage and do her bit. Right at the end of the number, she flung both her arms out with a gun in each hand. Her right hand held a pistol pointed directly at Hutchinson Smythe. And her left hand held one aimed directly at Harry S. Truman.

The song hit a crescendo and Ethel pulled both triggers. The guns popped loudly, accompanied by flashes and tiny puffs of smoke.

CHAPTER EIGHTEEN

A MOMENT AFTER THE GUNS EXPLODED, HUTCH'S ARM shot into the air.

Bunny turned in alarm, fear etched on her face. But Hutch clapped enthusiastically and seemed none the worse for wear. She looked over at the President. He, too, applauded wildly. She held the lorgnette up to her eyes and studied the President. There were no telltale signs of being hit by a gunshot. He was as robust and hearty as Hutch.

The cast took their final bows and disappeared behind the red velvet curtain.

Hutch gathered up his belongings, but Bunny remained seated as she watched the President put on his coat and walk out of the theater under his own steam. At least she wouldn't have to disappear into the underground tunnels.

***

Evangeline and Nigel had watched the finale of *Annie Get Your Gun* with matched concentration.

"Nothing happened."

"How could anything happen, Evie? You made me move the gun *just so* nothing would happen."

"I know. We did a good job. But did you notice who the star's guns were aimed at?"

"No." He hesitated. "I may have been dozing."

"Nigel, one of those guns was aimed directly at the President of the United States."

"Are you sure?"

"Yes. And the other one was aimed right at Bunny's new boyfriend."

"Lover would be more like it."

"But what good would he be to her dead?"

"True. If they were married, his death might be her ticket to easy street."

"She may have been paid to kill him," Evangeline reasoned. "Maybe she's not in love with him at all. Maybe she just got close to him so she could kill him."

"You may be onto something. Bunny's pretty calculating."

"And a leopard can't change its spots," Evangeline quipped.

"So it's murder for money. Either his money or someone else's."

"Yes, but ... unless she's working for someone else, she'd have nothing to gain from killing him now, because they're not married."

"So she was paid to kill him. Or the gun could have been meant for the President, in which case, congratulate yourself and pat me on the back. If that's what happened, we've just saved President Truman's life."

Later that evening, as they waited for their dinner to be served, Hutch praised the show they had just seen. "Ethel Merman is every bit as good as they say she is. Did you hear her belt out those songs? Her voice is probably still echoing in the rafters. Look. There's her caricature hanging on the wall."

They were sitting in a coveted red booth at Sardi's restaurant in the heart of the theater district. All around them were caricatures of major stars who had dined there previously, including Douglas Fairbanks and Ethel Barrymore.

"Hmm …" Bunny seemed preoccupied.

"Are you all right, Antonia? You were so excited about seeing the show this morning when you first told me you got tickets, but now, something is obviously troubling you."

"Oh, don't worry about me, darling. You know how women are, always fretting over some little thing or another."

"Put your worries away till morning. Tonight is a night for fun."

The waiter arrived, as if on cue, with a bottle of pink champagne and a bowl of iced strawberries.

Bunny forced a smile. "Hutch, you remembered."

He laughed. "How can I forget." He stretched across the table and kissed her. "I ordered them just for you, because you're so wonderful."

Bunny melted like a chocolate bar in the desert sun.

Hutch picked up his champagne glass. "May I propose a toast?"

"Darling, you can propose any little thing your heart desires."

"To us, Antonia. May this be the start of a long and fulfilling relationship."

The Imperial theater was completely empty except for the janitor sweeping out the stalls and two perplexed ghosts.

Evangeline poked around onstage looking for bullet casings. There were none to be found.

Meanwhile, Nigel investigated the private theater boxes used by Hutch and the President.

Evangeline joined him. "Are there any bullet holes in the President's box?"

"I don't see any."

"Then I guess we're done here."

"Where do you think Bunny and Hutch disappeared to?"

"Sardi's," Evangeline answered promptly. "He promised her an Alexander this afternoon."

"Right. I've been there, so I'll have no problem. How about you?"

"I've been there, as well. Let's go see what they're up to."

Hutch and Bunny held hands as they leaned across the table and gazed into each other's eyes. Hutch picked up a strawberry and fed it to Bunny. She closed her eyes and smiled as she savored its juicy sweetness. When she opened them, Hutch had leaned a little to his right, giving Bunny a clear view of the table directly behind him. Her eyes nearly bugged out of her head.

A lone diner held a menu, but instead of reading its offerings, he stared directly at her, his icy cold eyes boring into her brain. Even with his hat on, he had a familiar face. Too familiar. And he looked like he was about to spit bullets. Or worse.

CHAPTER NINETEEN

NIGEL MARVELED THAT THE ONLY THING THAT HAD changed at Sardi's since he'd last been there a decade earlier, was the number of caricatures of famous faces. The sketches not only graced the dark red walls above the matching banquettes, but also decorated the large square columns that structurally supported the crowded dining room.

All around him, people went about their daily business, including a man whom Lynn Fontanne had introduced Nigel to years before. His name was Brock Pemberton.

A famous stage actor hailed him. "Hey, Brock, how are you?" The actor extended his arm through Evangeline's ghostly spirit, forcing her to step out of his path as he continued his conversation. "I hear you want to create an award in Tony's name." He unconsciously rubbed his arm.

"Yeah, I've been talking it over with members of the American Theatre Wing. Just look at all the people who are pictured on these walls. They're all colleagues and friends of Tony's. She gave so much to them and the public, both on stage and off. And she was the best partner I could ever have hoped for. It was her idea to produce *Harvey*, and it's still going strong."

"So what are you planning?"

"Tony was an actress before she became a director and producer, so I'm thinking about asking Theatre Wing members to choose the season's best actors and actresses and the best shows and directors. We can give them scrolls with their names on them, or some similar token. And it's something we could do annually—like the Academy Awards out in Hollywood. We've been toying with the idea for a while and were thinking of calling it the American Theatre Wing awards. But after Tony died, members suggested doing something to honor *her*. So we're going to call them the Antoinette Perry awards."

"Sounds great, Brock, a real tribute to her memory. When can I expect my invitation?"

"Not for another year or so. We've got to work out the details first."

The man at the table next to Bunny and Hutch removed his hat. His hair had looked brown, but without the hat, it was obvious he had dark blond hair streaked with gray. A squared-off jaw with a cleft chin only showed a minimum of the slackness that comes with the passage of time. He wasn't young, but still appeared handsome, until you got close enough to see that his eyes reflected no warmth.

After her initial shock, Bunny did her best to pretend she hadn't seen him, but not convincingly.

"Antonia, are you sure you're all right?" Hutch asked.

"Of course, darling. My teeth are sensitive to cold and these strawberries are positively frigid. I'm just reacting to them."

"I'm sorry, darling. Would you like me to ask the management to warm them up?"

Bunny laughed. "No, I don't think that will be necessary. However, I can think of another way to 'warm' things up back at the hotel. Why don't we go?"

Hutch threw a hundred-dollar bill on the table and escorted Bunny out the door.

"Did you see that?"

"Yes," Evangeline answered. "I've never seen Bunny look that scared, although she did a good job of quickly covering it up. What do you think caused it?"

"It's not what. It's who. She was looking directly at that man at the next table."

"I can't see him from here."

Nigel grabbed Evangeline's hand, and they floated to the other end of the room. Evangeline couldn't believe her eyes. She felt her blood run cold. Or maybe it was just her ectoplasm freezing over.

Back at the Waldorf Astoria, Bunny did her best to entice Hutch, but knew her performance was sadly lacking.

"Darling, you look tired," Hutch told her. "Why don't you try to get some sleep?"

"What about you? Where are you going?"

"I'll be right on the other side of the door. I need to get some work done. The UN Security Council wants more details about my family's business ventures. I need to go through some paperwork and make a few phone calls."

"Darling, it's too late to make phone calls."

"Not for me. I'm making a lot of people rich, and if they want to continue being rich, they'll take my calls, no matter what time of the day or night it is. Now go rest your pretty little head, and I'll join you in an hour or so."

Bunny disappeared into the bedroom. She didn't like the idea of going to bed alone, but it would give her time to think. And she had a lot on her mind. Siegfried Feuermacht's appearance at Sardi's restaurant had unsettled her. And now that she knew he was in New York, she'd have to keep looking over her shoulder every other minute.

CHAPTER TWENTY

THE WALDORF ASTORIA THROBBED WITH ACTIVITY.

The Secret Service made arrangements for early room service, so the President's entourage could leave for the White House at dawn. Hotel staff buzzed around the president's men, making sure they overlooked no detail that involved the Commander in Chief's comfort. And several stories below, federal agents moved Truman's touring car to the siding of Track 61, so it could be loaded onto the *Ferdinand Magellan*—the private train that would take the president to Union Station in Washington, D.C.

The Secret Service's preparation to depart did not go unnoticed. An observer decided it was time to take a closer look at the President's transportation. There were so many people in the area, he obviously couldn't use the elevator just off the parking garage. It would be safer to enter through Grand Central Station and follow the rails to the siding.

Evangeline and Nigel didn't tail Bunny and Hutch back to their suite. Instead, they hung around the hotel lobby, eavesdropping on the President's travel plans. It certainly took a lot of work by a large number of people to move one man from New York to Washington, D.C.

It piqued Nigel's interest because the agents mapped it out like a military operation.

Evangeline was engrossed in the details, because she suspected Bunny might be trying to kill Truman, and she wanted to know his itinerary, so she could cut Bunny off at the pass.

It soon became evident that, aside from the unusual aspect of using the private train station beneath the hotel, the Secret Service did not have a contingency plan in place in the event of an assassination attempt. And since the agents didn't know about the gun at the theater, they had no reason to get their guard up.

What made it worse was that neither Nigel nor Evangeline had ever visited Track 61 when they were alive, so it was technically off-limits to them now.

"Let's go for a walk." Evangeline felt restless.

"Where do you want to go? We can probably transport ourselves there."

"I don't want to transport anywhere. I just want to walk."

"All right, if that helps."

"I need to think."

Grand Central Station was active at night, but not

as busy as during the day, so walking the rails to Track 61 was relatively easy.

The *Ferdinand Magellan* was a moving fortress that the Secret Service had the forethought to lock, even though it was on a private siding. The windows did not open, the door was bolted, and short of putting a bomb beneath the train and blasting a hole through it, the rail car was impenetrable.

However, the President's automobile was not as well protected, and it didn't take long to climb onto the siding, slide under the Lincoln convertible, and tamper with its brake line. It was just that simple.

After the ghostly duo circled the block for the fifth time, Nigel started fussing. He loved Evangeline dearly, but he was bored to tears. "If you're only going to walk around the block like this, I'll leave you to it. There are other things I could be doing that would be more effective than watching you think."

"Go," she replied, with a wave of her hand. "I'm perfectly fine out here alone."

He sighed with relief. Evangeline was preoccupied. She would never agree with what he planned to do. Just in case it didn't work out, he grabbed her and kissed her. He might as well leave a lasting impression. If his idea backfired, he might not get this opportunity again.

Surprisingly, Evangeline kissed him back with the same level of intensity.

"I'm glad to see you're willing to take a break from all this thinking that you're doing," he murmured, while gently tracing her lips with his kisses.

"I'm not taking a break. I can think while I kiss you, as easily as when I'm not kissing you."

"You really know how to make a guy feel special, Evie. I'll see you later." *Or maybe not.* He didn't really know.

EG.

CHAPTER TWENTY-ONE

BACK AT THE PEARLY GATES, SAINT PETER WAS AS BUSY as ever. It didn't matter that World War II had officially ended. A steady flow of humans who had suffered because of the extended conflict continued to find themselves at the divine depot. They were easy to identify—all skin and bones, with their clothing hanging from their skeletal bodies. There was a line for those who had starved to death, another line for people who hadn't been able to get the medicines they needed to fight the infections that ravaged their bodies, and a special line for the millions who had died after being tortured as medical guinea pigs.

Scores of people waited on every single line, and each line seemed to go on *forever*. Still, no one really looked like they cared. Those awaiting processing at the Pearly Gates suffered neither hunger nor pain.

Nigel waited patiently. He didn't need to

announce why he was there. Saint Peter already knew through the *Collective*. Nigel believed he'd be chastised for using telekinesis, or worse, prevented from rejoining Evangeline. He hoped that wouldn't happen, but it was something he was prepared to face.

"You can't change what's preordained."

Nigel jumped at the sound of Saint Peter's voice. He'd been so preoccupied with his own thoughts, he didn't realize the tall, bald man with the hooked nose now stood beside him. "I'm sorry, sir, but we don't really know what's preordained, do we? I mean, *you* might know, but for all Evie and I know, we may have been reunited back on earth to save the American President's life, or that of Hutchinson Smythe. We're really not sure which one yet."

"You know what the rules are about illegal emissions."

"Yes, sir, I know. I just tried to do the right thing. But I'm ready to accept whatever you decree. You didn't even have to send for me. I came on my own to accept my punishment."

"Enough already, stop being a martyr. Joan of Arc already cornered the market on that. I'm going to let you go back. Truman's time on earth isn't up yet. Neither is Smythe's. So I'm letting you continue your quest. But you've got to stop breaking the rules."

The light radiating from the skies above flickered.

"I stand corrected," Saint Peter continued. "You've got to stop allowing *Evangeline* to talk *you* into breaking the rules."

"I wouldn't have to go against regulations, sir, if you would give me a temporary special dispensation."

"I didn't make the rules, Nigel. I'm a man, just like

you, not a member of the Celestial Hierarchy. Unregulated emissions disturb the living, and the Hierarchy wants mortals to remain oblivious to what else is out here."

"Then we've got a problem, sir. One of the locations we need to access is out of bounds to us."

"There are ways around that, but it's not my place to tell you what they are. Petition the *Collective*, Nigel. They'll present it to the Hierarchy, and if they feel it's in the world's best interest for you to master a talent you don't currently have, that knowledge will be given to you."

"How do I petition the *Collective*, sir?"

Saint Peter tapped his right cheek with his forefinger. "It's done. Just remember to say 'please' and 'thank you.' They like that."

CHAPTER TWENTY-TWO

THE NEXT MORNING TURNED OUT TO BE ONE OF THOSE spectacular autumn days that people dream about. The air was fresh and crisp, and Central Park's mantle of red, yellow, and rust-colored leaves danced in the light breeze.

Inside the Waldorf Astoria, Truman's staff had everything packed and ready to go, but the President took his time—enjoying his breakfast on the balcony of his suite. He lingered over a second cup of coffee while he read the *New York Times*.

"Mr. President, we really need to get down to Track 61 if we don't want to create delays in the tunnels by making the morning trains wait for us to pass."

"I guess that wouldn't make the New York voters very happy."

"No, Mr. President. I'm sure the hotel wouldn't mind if we took your cup of coffee down to the platform with us. And, of course, you can continue reading the paper once we're onboard."

The President stood and placed his coffee cup on the table. "I'll be expecting fresh coffee onboard the *Ferdinand Magellan*. Just make sure this newspaper is placed next to my favorite chair."

"Good morning, Evie."

"Nigel, where have you been? I've been sitting here waiting for you."

"Why, what's going on?"

"It's nothing specific. Bunny is acting strangely."

"I should have known it would have something to do with Bunny." He sighed. "What's so odd about her today?"

"When I got back to the room in the wee hours of the morning, she was pacing back and forth and seemed agitated."

"Maybe she couldn't sleep."

"I'm sure she couldn't sleep. She was fully clothed."

"That doesn't mean anything. Fully clothed people fall asleep all the time. Haven't you ever been on the subway late in the evening?"

"She had on a girdle, Nigel. Women can't sleep in those. They're too constricting."

"Well, that's a deduction I would never have come up with on my own."

"I think we should go to the Presidential Suite."

"*This* is the Presidential Suite."

"Where's Truman?"

"In Astor's private suite."

"That's where we need to be."

"Have you ever been there?"

"Of course, it's right next door."

"Of course," Nigel mocked, under his breath.

But when they got there, the President was gone. Two maids worked quickly to ready it for its owner's return. John Jacob Astor IV had temporarily moved to a smaller suite to accommodate the President.

"We missed him." Evangeline moaned.

"Track 61," Nigel replied.

Sebastian Faust also checked out of the hotel. He had packed up his extensive wardrobe and settled his bill with the Waldorf Astoria before the sun had a chance to rise very high.

The hotel staff inquired if he was leaving because the room was inadequate. Faust made up an excuse about a sick grandchild and a worried daughter awaiting his arrival.

Truman arrived on the platform in time to see a group of men pushing his motorcar onto the train. "Why don't they save their backs and just drive the damn thing onboard?"

His Chief of Staff answered, "The man in charge of Track 61 apparently has asthma and started choking up a storm as soon as the car's motor turned over, so they shut it down. I believe their exact words were, 'We'll push *Old Bessie* onto the train.'"

The President laughed. "They'd better not let the First Lady hear them call that car 'Old Bessie' or we'll all be sorry."

He boarded the *Ferdinand Magellan*'s lounge

car and settled into an overstuffed wing chair, where he resumed reading the newspaper. He became so absorbed in the news of the day, he stopped paying attention to everything going on around him.

EG.

CHAPTER TWENTY-THREE

EVANGELINE AND NIGEL ARRIVED IN THE HOTEL PARKING garage just in time to see the President's entourage disappear into the elevator that would take them down to Track 61.

"Now what are we going to do?" Evangeline sighed. "I've never been to Track 61. Have you?"

"Just do what I tell you to do, Evie. Put your arms around me. I'm going to count to three, but instead of saying three, we're both going to say 'Deus vult' at the exact same moment."

"What will that do?"

"Just do it, okay?"

She put her arms around him. "I'm ready."

"Okay. One. Two. Deus vult."

Nigel disappeared right out of her arms. Evangeline looked around for him, but he was gone.

A moment later, he returned. "Evie, you were supposed to say 'Deus vult' with me."

"Can we do it again?"

"If it works again. Are you ready?"

"Yes. Deus vult. I'm ready."

She wrapped her arms around Nigel, again. This time she recited the words on cue, and they instantly transported to the siding of Track 61.

Surprisingly, Bunny and Hutch were standing less than ten feet away.

"Boy, those two sure get around," Nigel noted as both he and Evangeline stared at the couple. "What do you think they're up to now?"

"I don't know, but I think it's safe to say the President's safety is at risk."

"We haven't established that yet, Evie. Bunny could be after Smythe's fortune. Maybe she's here to conveniently bump up against him—sending him sprawling onto the tracks just as the President's train begins to move."

"Do you really think that's going to happen?"

"I don't know what's going to happen any more than you do. All we can do is look, listen, and learn until we find something amiss."

The door to the railroad car carrying the President's armor-plated Lincoln slammed shut and a Secret Service officer bolted it. He gave the engineer a two-finger salute before calling out, "All aboard."

The White House aide, who had been speaking with Hutchinson Smythe, shook his hand quickly, nodded at Bunny, and boarded the train.

At that point, Evangeline did not know what to

do. She looked to Nigel for an answer.

"It will be fine, Evie. There's no reason to suspect foul play."

The train pulled away and as it moved, Evangeline could see between the individual cars to the other side of the platform. She saw a man skulking away. "Nigel, there's someone suspicious on the other side of the train. Look between the cars."

The ghosts witnessed his countenance for only a moment when he turned to looked at the moving train, but it was enough time to make a positive identification.

"Siegfried Feuermacht," Evangeline gasped. "What if *he* sabotaged the train?"

"Quick, Evie, remember, say 'Deus vult' instead of three." Nigel grabbed her hand. "One … two … Deus vult."

Suddenly, they found themselves onboard the lounge car of the *Ferdinand Magellan*, just a few feet from the President.

The car's interior impressed Evangeline. It had a comfortable sitting room, where every window was dressed with blinds and framed by curtains. The President relaxed in one of several upholstered chairs, but could work if he wanted to at a writing desk tucked against the rear wall. An oak-paneled dining room with a large mahogany table and chairs sat at the opposite end of the car with an attached pantry and galley. Two guest rooms and a Presidential Suite with its own bathroom linked the more public spaces.

"Look at these," Evangeline said, pointing to brass wall sconces. "And there's a bathtub onboard. I wouldn't mind traveling like this."

"Are we here to admire the interior, or look for signs of sabotage?"

"I hate it when you're right. The least you could do is pretend to be curious. Where do you think we should begin?"

"I don't know, but I would guess the undercarriage of the train would be the best place to start. He may have planted a bomb or grenade there."

"How do we do that on a moving train?"

Nigel knelt down and pushed his head and shoulders through the solid floor of the carriage, to see if anything looked out of place.

Evangeline stared at him in amazement. *Why didn't I think of that?*

He finished his task and pulled his head back into the car. "There's nothing under this car, but there are a few more cars to check, so let's move on to the next one."

They checked out a sleeper car for the President's staff, followed by a communications car; both proved to be free of any obvious signs of sabotage.

Nigel moved to the car carrying the President's Lincoln convertible. The undercarriage of the train showed no ominous additions, but as Nigel raised his head up past the floorboards, he noticed a tiny bit of fluid on the floor. Taking a closer look, he realized the Lincoln's brake line was dripping. The hose looked like a nail or an awl had punctured it. He turned to Evangeline. "I do believe someone has sabotaged the President's car."

EL

CHAPTER TWENTY-FOUR

BUNNY AND HUTCH SAT DOWN TO LUNCH AT OSCAR'S in the Waldorf Astoria. Bunny had forfeited thoughts of wearing something that hugged her curves and had donned a sedate mid-calf sheath of royal blue wool. She wore her hair twisted in a fashionable chignon and subdued makeup. She looked elegant and tried her best to act the same way.

Her attention to detail was not lost on Hutch, who told her more than once he thought she looked beautiful.

Still, during dessert, he surprised her. "You know I adore you, Antonia."

"Darling, what a sweet thing to say."

Hutch took her hand and slipped a tiny blue box into it.

Bunny's heart thumped. She felt almost girlish. She had shunned romantic notions for years, using men only to get what she wanted, never giving them an opportunity to trample her heart. Now, she realized that she had fallen in love—something she had promised herself she would never do. It didn't hurt that the object of her affections was rich and handsome.

She opened the box slowly. She hoped for a ring, but knew that would be unlikely since they barely knew each other. Instead, he had given her an exquisite pair of diamond-and-sapphire earrings worth a small fortune. She didn't want to say, "Hutch, you shouldn't have …" because he might take her at her word and never give her anything again. She couldn't comment about their obvious value, because even though she was overwhelmed by what they might be worth, his family owned diamond and sapphire mines and probably thought of these as a mere token. She had no idea what the appropriate response should be, so she simply said, "Thank you, I'll treasure them always." She realized, by Hutch's reaction, that she had stumbled upon the right answer.

"I thought of giving you a ring, but I didn't want to scare you away."

Bunny tried to remain calm and kept her voice light. "You couldn't scare me away, Hutch, no matter how hard you tried."

"That's what I love about you, Antonia. You always say the right thing. But you'd better not give me false hope," he continued. "I might pop the question, prematurely."

Could she believe her ears? "What question is that?" she asked, coyly.

"The one where I ask you to marry me. You know, nothing would make me happier."

Bunny nearly choked on her pink champagne. "Of course I'll marry you, darling. I'd marry you this instant, if there was a magistrate in the room."

"You know, Antonia, I think there is. Mayor William O'Dwyer is sitting right over there." He nodded in the direction of the Mayor's table. "Should I ask him if he would officiate?"

"I think that's a brilliant idea."

"Are you sure? It would be a simple ceremony. No big church wedding with all the fancy trappings."

"I don't need a fancy wedding, Hutch. I just need you." Her smile was genuine.

"Then that settles it. I'm going to go ask him, right now."

Hutch approached the Mayor and spoke with him for only a few minutes, finally returning to Bunny with the Mayor in tow.

For Bunny, it had seemed like an eternity, and the sight of the Mayor approaching filled her with both pleasure and apprehension.

Faust felt ill at ease. He had made it a point to stay out of Bunny's way on the train platform and was pretty sure she hadn't seen him. But he knew by the look on her face the previous night that she had recognized him as Siegfried Feuermacht, and he didn't want her to spoil his plan. However, *wishing* Bunny out of the picture was not enough. He'd have to find a way to make sure they would never cross paths again.

Until the previous evening, he had enjoyed virtual anonymity, with most of the world believing him dead. The *special project* he had allowed himself to be subjected to—in the name of the Reich—had been a highly guarded secret that few people were privy to. He had never heard of cloning until he joined the Nazi party, and not even the Führer knew he had taken part in "an experiment."

A wave of sadness wash over him. His biggest regret had been asking Sigmund to impersonate him when he needed to close an account at Bank Liu in Bern eight years ago. It seemed like a simple task at the time, but the Nazis intercepted Sigmund and, thinking he was Siegfried, had killed him. Feuermacht had been bereft, but kept telling himself that Sigmund had served his main purpose in life by benefitting his benefactor.

It had all started with Feuermacht's introduction to Dr. Felix Wetzstein.

"What is the subject of your research, Dr. Wetzstein?"

"Biological cell reproduction."

"Babies? Or are you researching cancer?"

"Neither. I'm conducting experiments into creating genetic duplicates of living things, using their own cells."

"Plants?"

"Animals."

"Mice?"

"Humans."

"People!"

"Shhh … Herr Feuermacht. Please keep your voice down. There are some who do not think very highly of scientists who—they claim—are trying to play God. Maybe you are one of them?"

"No, quite the contrary. I'm very interested in what you are trying to do. Have you actually been able to

reproduce a human being?"

"I'm working on it. There are officials who believe producing an army of perfect German soldiers would help the Reich achieve world supremacy."

"I see. You're planning for the future."

"For the very near future."

"It couldn't be that 'near.' Surely, it would take a generation for your reproductions to grow."

"I have been working on a special amino-acid solution that helps cells develop more rapidly and grow four times as quickly."

"You've tested this?"

"Only on mice, but I'm getting ready to experiment on something larger."

"Doctor. Your research intrigues me. Would it be possible for me to tour your facility?"

"Oh. It's not much, Herr Feuermacht, I assure you—just a bunch of petri dishes, beakers, and micro-scopes. But if you're really interested, I have some free time tomorrow."

"Excellent."

The doctor fished through his pockets, seeking a scrap of paper. He took a pen and scribbled the location. "Here's the address."

"Thank you, Doctor. I look forward to seeing you again."

The next morning, Feuermacht agreed that the facilities were modest, but that didn't make the prospects any less interesting. It helped that the doctor used simple language to explain the procedure.

"So are you saying, Dr. Wetzstein, that if I give you

a drop of my blood, you would be able to replicate me?"

"No, Herr Feuermacht. I would need to extract some bone marrow. I would have to penetrate your breastbone with a large needle to get a sample."

"Wouldn't that be like stabbing me in the heart?"

"Not if a skilled scientist, like myself, were to do it. Granted, it's not an easy extraction. Any patient would be discomforted for weeks."

"But the outcome could be tremendous."

"Yes."

"I would like to volunteer myself."

"Excuse me?"

"I would like to submit to the extraction process. Of course, certain considerations would have to be met."

"Such as?"

"Considering this replica would have my imprint, I would like some say in its future."

"You do realize, Herr Feuermacht, that this is experimental, and as such, the product may not live long enough to have any sort of future?"

"But if it were successful, it is small payment in return for the contribution my bone marrow would make to your research."

"That is true."

"Then, Doctor, all you have to do is extract what you need."

"When would you like to do this?"

"Right now."

Dr. Wetzstein hesitated, even though he knew getting another donor would not be easy, but quickly reined in his reluctance. "Please remove your jacket and shirt, Herr Feuermacht. I'll be right back."

The doctor dragged a heavy chair into his lab. "Have a seat."

"A chair isn't necessary. I can stand."

"You don't understand, Herr Feuermacht. As you said before, this could be like getting stabbed in the heart. That is what we must avoid. To ensure success, I must bind you to the chair so you can't move."

"I see." Feuermacht reluctantly sat down. Suddenly, the extraction of bone marrow was not as simple as it had originally sounded.

The doctor used bandages to attach Feuermacht's arms and legs to the chair. He was much heavier than Feuermacht and used his own belt to secure his donor's waist to the chair's splat. Wetzstein pressed his fingers into Feuermacht's chest. When he found the spot where he needed to insert the needle, he took a small piece of surgical tape and marked the spot. "I am going to use ether to make you unconscious."

"No."

"This is a very exacting and painful procedure, Herr Feuermacht, and it's necessary that you do not move. The ether will help us to that end."

"I demand to be aware of what's going on. No ether."

"Very well. In that case, I'd better give you something to bite on. You're going to need it." He twisted a cotton bandage into a long coil and placed it between Feuermacht's teeth. "Are you ready?"

Feuermacht nodded.

Wetzstein picked up a large syringe, placed his left hand on Feuermacht chest, and punched the needle into the man's breastbone with a twisting motion. Feuermacht's body went rigid as he involuntarily groaned in pain. The *coiled bandage muffled the sound.*

"I told you this would be painful, Herr Feuermacht, and we may have to insert the syringe several times to get a sufficient amount of bone marrow." He slowly pulled the plunger on the syringe and watched as it filled with thick red tissue. Wetzstein removed the needle and Feuermacht gasped for breath through his nose. Before he had finished taking the breath, Wetzstein had plunged another needle slightly to the left of the first puncture mark. A stream of blood squirted from Feuermacht's chest, staining the doctor's white shirt.

Another strangled groan escaped the patient as he bit so violently on the bandage, he felt certain he had bitten right through it. The doctor extracted more spongy tissue before removing the second syringe. He allowed minimal time to elapse before jamming a third needle into Feuermacht's chest. He quickly extracted a third vial of bone marrow, and placed the syringe next to the others on a metal tray.

Feuermacht's face had turned nearly purple.

"We are done. You need to rest now, Herr Feuermacht," Wetzstein said, as he picked up a gauze sponge and soaked it with ether. "This will help."

When Feuermacht awakened, he found himself lying on an army cot, left over from the Great War. His head throbbed, but so did his chest, and he scarcely moved. Another involuntary groan alerted the doctor that his patient had awakened.

"Herr Feuermacht, it is good to see that you have rejoined the living."

"My chest …"

"It will be sore for a few weeks until it completely heals, but I assure you, aside from the pain, you are in excellent health."

"My head …"

"Yes, ether does that, but the residual effects will wear off soon, now that you are awake. It was best to administer the ether, so I could clean the puncture wounds without submitting you to any more misery. Please do not remove the bandage. It has been treated with iodine to help the healing process."

"My bone marrow …"

"The quality is superb. I have isolated several cells, and they are soaking in a nutrient-rich elixir in a petri dish. I still need to extract egg cells from another donor before I can continue with the experiment, but those should be easier to get.

"If you come back in a few days, Herr Feuermacht, you can watch as we introduce the nuclei from your cells to egg cells that have had their own nuclei removed."

"And then what happens?"

"We experiment using different combinations of hormones and amino acids to stimulate cell growth. If any one of them is successful, we will need a host mother to carry the fetus to term."

"How difficult is it to find someone to do that?"

"Unfortunately, Herr Feuermacht, I cannot answer that question, because we have never had the occasion to need someone. But there are plenty of impoverished women in this city, and I'm sure we'll find a host if we pay her well enough."

Cells taken from Feuermacht's first vial of bone marrow met with only limited success. They didn't survive, *but they did teach Wetzstein and his colleagues what not to do.*

The second vial of bone marrow had more success; however, the embryos developed too rapidly and mutated.

It was only months later, when Wetzstein worked on the last refrigerated vial of Feuermacht's bone marrow, that he found a way to control the cells' growth. He scrambled to find a "mother." In the end, the doctor implanted the embryo in his wife's womb, for the sake of discretion and privacy.

Feuermacht insisted his replica be called Sigmund—a variation of his own name. Wetzstein and his wife raised the boy, although they were forced to move often to avoid having to explain why their child grew so much faster than normal. To Feuermacht, the boy was like a favorite toy. He visited often to witness his clone's progress, and they formed a strong attachment.

Feuermacht put Sigmund out of his mind. He needed to hatch a new plan. Bunny had looked pretty cozy with Hutchinson Smythe. They'd held hands and gazed into each other's eyes, and every so often, Bunny had leaned against Smythe to whisper in his ear and then giggle. Never in his life had Feuermacht expected to see Bunny *giggle*. He hated the very idea of it.

His first thought involved Smythe having a horrible *accident*, which might divert Bunny's attention. But, more likely than not, she'd smell a rat and would turn all her might against him.

His only alternative was to eliminate Bunny altogether. That could be tricky with Smythe in the picture, because he had unlimited resources and might launch an investigation to determine if his *beloved* Antonia had met with foul play.

Her death would have to appear natural: an illness, perhaps? What could he use that would make her deadly ill? Curare? Strychnine? Hemlock? He would have to research his murder method, very carefully.

Nigel dipped his finger into the brake fluid and sniffed it, to make sure that's what it was. "This has to be deliberate."

"How can you be sure?"

"Because it's not a natural tear in the line. It's a perfect little hole. It probably wouldn't matter the first time the President's driver stepped on the brake, but after that, there would be too little brake fluid to effectively stop the car a second time."

"We need to stop President Truman from using this car." Evangeline paused, lost in thought. "In the meantime, you'd better have a look at the bottoms of the baggage cars and the engine, just to make sure there's nothing planted under them."

EG.

CHAPTER TWENTY-FIVE

FEUERMACHT CROUCHED DOWN BY AN HERBACEOUS border at the Brooklyn Botanic Gardens.

"I wouldn't touch that if I were you." The shadow of a gardener crossed Feuermacht's path.

"It reminds me of a border in my aunt's garden, back home."

"Maybe, but the Palma Christi can be quite poisonous, which is why all those signs are posted that say 'Danger. Do not touch.'"

A rowdy group of children ran past, nearly knocking Feuermacht over. "I'm sorry," he said as he stood up. "I thought that was just your way of saying don't pick the flowers."

"No. It is what it says."

"I see."

"From the sound of your accent, I'd say you're a

long way from home. What brings you to the Botanic Gardens?"

Feuermacht laughed. "Actually, I'm here on holiday and I've developed a bit of a stomach problem. I've been having a difficult time finding castor beans so I can extract a little of the oil."

"You can buy castor oil in pharmacies."

"I don't believe in using products that are mass-produced. You can never really be sure of the potency or know how long it's been sitting on a shelf."

A screaming child made them turn their heads, but didn't interrupt the conversation.

"So instead, you'd rather make your own castor oil?"

"Yes."

"And you know how to extract the oil from the beans?" The gardener sounded skeptical.

"It's an old family tradition. I grew up in a small village in … Switzerland, where you made your own, or you did without."

"Well, we've got castor plants here, but they're at the back end of the border, out of the reach of the general public. And like all the vegetation here, the sign that says 'Danger. Do not touch' applies to them, as well."

"Humph. Do you know where I can buy some castor beans?"

"Maybe one of those little markets in Chinatown. They've always got an odd assortment of plants and seeds."

Several children ran through a flower bed and distracted the gardener. "Stop! You get out of there, this instant!" He stormed off to reprimand the youngsters.

Feuermacht quickly pulled on a leather glove, stepped over the herbaceous border, and grabbed a handful of castor seeds. He pulled off the glove, turning it inside out to create a makeshift bag for the seeds inside, and stuffed it in his pocket, escaping before the gardener had a chance to return.

The *Ferdinand Magellan* displayed no further signs of sabotage. "I think the car is our smoking gun, Evie."

"Well, we've got to do something to stop them from driving it. What would call attention to this?"

"Perhaps a bigger puddle of fluid."

"We still couldn't be sure they would notice it."

"So what do you want me to do? Lean a big sign against the car that says 'The brake line has been sabotaged'?"

"You're right, Nigel. That would certainly call their attention to it."

"But it's beyond our capabilities."

"Why can't you use telekinesis to move it?"

"I can't move something that's attached."

"Well, then. We have to disable the car in some way."

"We may be able to give it a flat tire."

"How?"

"I can probably use telekinesis to press a small object like a pencil against the tire valve, letting the air escape."

"But don't stop at one tire. Do it to all four tires, that way, they'll definitely suspect something and discover the problem with the brake line."

"That is more easily said than done."

"Antonia," Hutch said proudly, "the Mayor has agreed to marry us tomorrow at Gracie Mansion."

"Lady Antonia, it's an honor to meet you." The Mayor took Bunny's hand.

Bunny blushed. No one had ever called meeting her "an honor."

Hutch slipped his arm around Bunny's shoulders. "Isn't she a gem?" He leaned over and kissed her cheek before saying to the Mayor, "We'll be there at high noon."

"Wonderful," O'Dwyer answered. "And if you would allow me, I'd like to host a small luncheon immediately afterward, for you and your wonderful bride."

"We'd be honored."

Bunny remained speechless.

"Such a sweet woman"—the Mayor directed his comment at Hutch—"but shy."

O'Dwyer turned to Bunny. "We're going to have to work on making you a little more outgoing."

She smiled. *If he only knew.*

CHAPTER TWENTY-SIX

HUTCH TUCKED A BANKROLL INTO BUNNY'S PURSE AND told her to go buy herself something pretty to wear to the wedding. He had a few things to attend to, and said he would meet her back at the Waldorf Astoria in time for dinner.

He walked her down to the concierge. "Peter, I want you to hire a limousine for Lady Antonia that will take her to the best stores in town. And have the driver wait for her wherever she goes, until she's done—even if it takes all afternoon.

"Goodbye, my love." Hutch kissed her cheek before walking away.

Bunny's first stop: Bergdorf Goodman.

She had only been inside Bergdorf's once before, with her cousin Lynn, who needed a cocktail dress for the opening-night party for one of her Broadway shows. At the time, Bunny thought the clothes were as snooty as the women who bought them. But she had to admit that Lynn looked like a class act in the gown she had chosen. And since meeting Hutchinson Smythe, Bunny's tastes had changed along with her name. She was now ready to become a Bergdorf customer—and a regular one at that.

The store sat on Fifth Avenue between 57th and 58th Streets, which had once been the site of the largest residence ever built in Manhattan—the Cornelius Vanderbilt mansion. But taxes on the home had been astronomical, and Bergdorf Goodman had purchased the property in the 1920s, demolished the mansion, and built its new store there. Now, nearly two decades later, the store had become an exclusive destination for high fashion.

As soon as she announced her impending nuptials to the ultra-rich Hutchinson Smythe, store personnel bent over backwards to make sure *Lady Antonia Southerland* ended the day as a satisfied customer. They seated her on a velvet divan and brought the fashions to her. After making several preliminary selections, Bunny disappeared into a dressing room, where she spent an hour trying on outfits.

By the time she left, Bunny owned a new cream-colored silk suit with a nipped-in waist and a matching coat that had an oversized Mongolian lamb collar that draped over her shoulders. A complementary felt beret, matching gloves, taupe shoes and a clutch filled a huge shopping bag. And she had splurged on a lacy peignoir to wear on her wedding night, along with a pair of velvet mules with marabou trim.

Bunny spent every dime Hutch had given her, and then some. She refused to leave the store without a pair of white pearl earrings to wear at her wedding. And when the sales staff spread the word on the identity of the groom, the management eagerly opened a charge account in Lady Southerland's name, so she could continue her shopping spree.

Feuermacht also went shopping. He searched through several small stores that sold housewares and pharmaceuticals before finding a mortar and pestle in the bottom of a box of used kitchen utensils. He threw a few dollars down on the counter and rushed out of the store. It may have been more than the items were worth, but he didn't want to give anyone enough time to memorize his face.

Crushing the seeds would be a simple task. Finding a way to poison Bunny with their residue so it would be undetectable might be more difficult. He didn't want to arouse her suspicion. He just wanted her to think she had a cold. The last thing he wanted to do was give her a reason to become apprehensive and seek medical attention.

He returned to the fleabag hotel he had checked into after leaving the Waldorf Astoria. This hotel didn't have the same amenities, but the anonymity it afforded him was priceless.

Back in his room, he meticulously crushed the castor beans and squeezed out the oil. The greasy liquid was expendable, but the poisonous mash that remained was just what the doctor ordered—the doctor of death, that is. He worked the mash into a fine paste and scraped it into a small glass jar. He wouldn't need much for a lethal dose. He only had to get Bunny to swallow it.

He could already imagine the outcome. At first, she would think she had the flu. But she wouldn't get better. And in the end, her cells would stop producing protein, her organs would cease to function, and Bunny Stanton—*or whatever her name is*—would die.

He checked the hallway to make sure it was empty before carrying the mortar and pestle to the bathroom to wash them. It would have been more convenient to dispose of the set, but he might need it again. Afterward, he showered, just to make sure no traces of the castor-bean residue remained on his skin. Then, he grabbed his jacket and went out for a walk.

Feuermacht didn't head anywhere in particular. Walking engaged his thought processes, and he needed to devise a plan to poison Bunny. He had been walking for hours when the aroma of chocolate teased his olfactory glands. He found himself standing outside a confectionery shop, where he could see a woman making chocolate candies through the window. He ventured inside. A long row of dark brown cabinets with bulbous glass windows showed off platters of freshly made sweets. The floorboards creaked as he made his way across the dull wooden surface to the back of the store, where the proprietor worked.

"Do you mind if I watch?"

"Would you like to purchase some of my bonbons?" Sophie Morel had an accent as thick as her eyeglasses. She wiped her hands on her full-length apron, already smeared with various shades of chocolate.

"Is that what you're making?"

"Yes. My customers can't get enough of them. They keep me busy making bonbons day and night."

He watched her mix butter and powdered sugar together, and then add condensed milk and shredded coconut. When the thick mixture reached the consistency she wanted, she rolled pieces of it into one-inch balls and placed them on a tray.

"Is that all there is to it?"

"Oh, no. Once they've set for a few hours, I'll dip them in melted chocolate. Women can't resist chocolate." She laughed. "The trick is to add a little paraffin to it. It makes the coating glisten. You watch."

She took a large slab of chocolate and smacked it against the counter, breaking it into pieces. She placed the broken bits into a double boiler, along with a small chunk of paraffin. When the waxy chocolate mixture had melted, she took a tray of bonbons from the refrigerator, skewered each piece on a long metal pin, dipped it in the chocolate, and then placed it on a tray covered with waxed paper.

If she could peek inside Feuermacht's mind, she would have seen the wheels of his imagination turning.

"I'd like to buy the plain bonbons you just made—the ones without the chocolate."

"Oh, no, sir. They're not ready."

He smiled at her. "I have a lady friend. I would like her to think that I am making these candies just for her. If you would sell me the unfinished bonbons, and bars of chocolate and paraffin, I can invite her over to help me put the finishing touches on the candies. I believe your bonbons will put her in a very amorous mood, no?

"And I'll pay whatever price you ask. I'd like to

buy a box of your beautifully finished bonbons, as well. Those will be for me," he said with a wink.

"What men won't do to get their way with the ladies," she said, laughing. "As you wish."

She wrapped everything in white paper and tied it with ribbon.

Now it was Feuermacht's turn to laugh. He had what he believed to be a foolproof plan.

John Cullen needed the duty roster for the *Ferdinand Magellan* so he could finish his paperwork. He hated filing reports, but he only had two more months of bureaucratic red tape to wade through before retiring. He had been with the Secret Service for twenty-five years and looked forward to, what he called, his *afterlife*.

John protected the President of the United States for a living. He took his job seriously and was very good at it. But he had grown up in Amagansett, New York, on the southern coast of Long Island and he wanted to settle there with his family and invest in a fishing boat. A lot of people paid good money for the chance to sail the Atlantic Ocean and hook a mako shark, and John thought there was no better way to spend the rest of his days than getting paid to do something he loved.

Maybe he'd even invite President Truman to go out on his boat, one day. But for now, he still had to prepare his report for Frank Wilson, the chief of the Secret Service.

Nigel looked all through the boxcar, but couldn't find anything suitable to use on the valves.

"Maybe we could get a knife from the kitchen,"

Evangeline mused.

"And transport it between moving railroad cars? I don't think so."

They were interrupted by John Cullen's entrance.

"Look, Nigel, he has a pen sticking out of his breast pocket. Grab it."

"You really don't understand what a delicate operation it is to move an object and not be seen."

"We may never get another opportunity. You don't want President Truman to die, do you?"

Evangeline always seemed to know which turn of a phrase would spur Nigel to action.

"He'll see me."

"Yes. But who will believe him?"

Hmm … She had a point.

Nigel watched John grab a clipboard hanging on a nail near the Lincoln and jot down a few notes. As John stuffed the pen back in his pocket, Nigel used telekinesis to ruffle the papers on the clipboard. The agent turned to see where the breeze originated, and Nigel lifted the pen from his pocket.

John turned back when he heard another agent entering from the opposite end of the boxcar.

"Hey, John," the agent called out, "did you call the secretary when we stopped for fuel?"

John didn't answer. Instead, he stood rooted to the floor, mesmerized by the sight of his green marbleized Inkograph fountain pen floating in midair.

Nigel let the pen drop and kicked it under the car.

CHAPTER TWENTY-SEVEN

FEUERMACHT WORE RUBBER GLOVES TO MIX HIS homemade ricin into the unfinished bonbons. He worked quickly, mashing a little poison into the flesh of each candy, and then rolling it back into shape.

While he worked, chocolate and paraffin melted in a tin pan, precariously balanced over a Bunsen burner. Feuermacht coated a couple of candies. They didn't look as tempting as the ones from the candy store, which bothered him.

Maybe if I sprinkled a little coconut on top, it will disguise the amateur look of this candy. But that meant he would have to go out and buy coconut, which presented a problem. He hadn't chosen a very secure hotel and he was afraid to leave everything out in the open where prying eyes might invite trouble.

He shoved everything under the bed in a

haphazard attempt to hide it all. It really wouldn't help if someone came in looking for a quick score, but at least he had hidden it from plain sight. He stuffed some pillows under a blanket to make it look like he was asleep, and made sure a sheet dipped down over the side of the bed to obscure the contraband.

He climbed out the window onto a fire escape, and left the hotel through the alley.

"What's wrong, John? You look like you saw a ghost." The other agent seemed concerned.

Ironically, John hadn't seen a ghost at all. Nigel's telekinetic skills were improving, which kept his emissions to a minimum. But even though John didn't see Nigel, he did see his pen floating in the air, and then witnessed its erratic journey to a region beneath the President's touring car.

"Did you see that?" John asked softly.

"I'm not sure what you're talking about."

"Did you see my pen?"

"Not since you signed the duty roster with it. Why? Did you lose it?"

"No ... Yes! I must have misplaced it." John quickly changed the subject. "Were you looking for me?"

"Yeah. I just asked you if you made that call to Washington when we stopped to refuel."

"I did, but I don't have my notes with me. They're in Car Number One."

"Well, c'mon. Let's get them. We're already on the outskirts of Philly."

"That was close. Too close," Nigel admitted after

the two men left the boxcar. "If I could sweat, I'd be wringing out my shirt."

"I saw you kick the pen under the car. You kicked it, Nigel. That wasn't telekinesis. How did you do that?"

"I don't know. I think the *Collective* intervened."

"Are you sure? Maybe it's a new talent that you developed."

"It doesn't matter, Evie. It's against the rules. It's not a talent we're supposed to be using. "

"Rules. Rules. Rules. I'm so sick of the godforsaken rules. It's not like we're doing this for a bit of sport, Nigel. We're trying to save the President's life."

"And that's the only reason why you two are still here," a voice thundered.

Nigel and Evangeline both jumped. They hadn't expected Saint Peter to hitch a ride on the *Ferdinand Magellan*.

Climbing up the fire escape proved to be more difficult than Feuermacht's initial descent. His weight had forced the escape ladder to lower itself to the street, but the counterweight had made it retract out of his reach. He had no alternative but to enter the hotel through the lobby. Suddenly, switching to this fleabag hotel no longer seemed like a good idea. The small lobby had so little business that Feuermacht knew the bored clerk would wonder how a man he hadn't seen leave, could return. A diversion would be necessary.

He walked to the street corner and stopped by a trash bin, where he searched inside his pockets for a bit of detritus to discard. He nonchalantly surveyed the area until his fingers closed on the receipt from the chocolate shop. When no one was looking, he threw it away and pulled the fire alarm affixed to a neighboring light pole. Then he ducked down an alley, where he waited.

It took fire trucks more than ten minutes to arrive on the scene. When they did, everyone poured out of the surrounding buildings, including his hotel, to see what was going on. Feuermacht used the distraction to blend into the crowd until an opportune time when he could slip inside.

Back in his room, he coated the bonbons with chocolate and sprinkled them with coconut. They looked much more appealing. They would look even better when he placed them in the box that currently held Sophie's *finished* bonbons.

He popped one of her professionally made candies into his mouth and chewed it slowly. The delicate confection made him sigh. He hoped the ricin in his doctored candies didn't overwhelm their flavor. He wanted Bunny to enjoy each and every one of them.

The poisoned bonbons looked perfect inside the confectionery box. Feuermacht rewrapped it in the original white paper and ribbon. He just needed to deliver them. Bunny would take care of the rest.

Nigel and Evangeline did not need to explain their actions. Saint Peter already knew. It took a simple blink of his eyes and all four tires on the President's Lincoln went flat. To be on the safe side, Saint Peter also twirled his forefinger and the brake hose stretched out noticeably from beneath the car.

The Secret Service men would not be happy when they noticed it, but at least the President would be assured a safe arrival.

Saint Peter nodded, and Evangeline and Nigel found themselves standing in the middle of a dense white fog.

"Where are we?"

Nigel rubbed the back of his neck. "I don't even want to guess."

CHAPTER TWENTY-EIGHT

EVANGELINE AND NIGEL FOUND THEMSELVES TOGETHER but alone amid fingers of gray mist that appeared to point at them in a reproachful manner. They could see no light source, yet darkness remained at bay, and it felt neither warm nor cold.

"Nigel, there's no floor."

"I know."

Evangeline squinted. "No ceiling either. Not even sky. At least the Pearly Gates had some semblance of sky."

"Yeah."

"And we're just hanging here."

"Weightless, just like the agent's pen on the *Ferdinand Magellan*."

"Do you think we're in Limbo?"

"I don't think so."

"Then where are we?"

Nigel hesitated before answering. "I believe we're in a holding cell, awaiting a hearing before the Celestial Hierarchy."

"This is all my fault."

"Don't blame yourself, Evie. I wouldn't have done all those things if I didn't really want to. I'm as culpable as you are."

"How long do you think we'll have to wait?"

"The Celestial Hierarchy doesn't punch a time clock. We'll simply remain here until we're summoned to appear before them."

"In the meantime, Bunny may kill the President."

"If it's meant to be, we have no right interfering."

"But didn't Saint Peter say that President Truman's time isn't up yet?"

"That was then, this is now. Just because he wasn't supposed to die in the theater doesn't mean he wasn't supposed to die today in a car accident."

"We already know he wasn't, or else Saint Peter wouldn't have made the tires go flat."

"True." Nigel sighed. "I guess we just broke too many rules trying to protect him. Don't forget, that Secret Service agent saw his pen hovering before I could kick it under the car."

"Did you figure out how you did that?"

"The *Collective* thing apparently disseminates critical information, like how to propel an object, on a need-to-know basis. And I guess at that moment I needed to know."

"Could you do it again?"

"It doesn't matter. I don't think we'll ever get another chance to find out."

"How bad can Limbo be?"

"I'm thinking Hell, Evie."

Her eyes widened. "They wouldn't."

"They would. They could. They can."

The two of them contemplated their own thoughts and fears, growing quiet as the mist swirled around them.

The silence didn't last long. Evangeline's soft singing pulled Nigel out of his reverie. She sang one of the numbers from *Annie Get Your Gun*, and as time passed, her singing grew louder. She was no Ethel Merman, but she could certainly belt out a tune.

The mist took on a bright blue light and spun itself into the visage of a man of blinding beauty.

Evangeline stopped singing. "Are you God?" The question sounded almost childlike.

No. I am a Principality of the Third Sphere.

Evangeline and Nigel both stared at him. Even though they heard him quite clearly, his lips never moved.

"What are we supposed to do?" Evangeline asked.

I'm here to escort you to the Court of the Dominions.

"Both of us?"

In time. Right now, I've come for Nigel.

Before she could say another word, Evangeline was alone.

Gray skies didn't dampen Bunny's spirits. It was her wedding day and she had scads of details to attend to. She had an appointment to get her hair styled and her nails manicured at the Waldorf Astoria's beauty salon. The manager said she would have to wait until nine o'clock because they couldn't take her any earlier. She repeatedly proclaimed her title while she argued that she was marrying *Hutchinson Smythe*, and needed an earlier appointment. She insisted the manager give her preferential treatment because, as she stated emphatically, "The Mayor is hosting the ceremony and reception himself."

However, the salon manager would not be cowed. "It's too late to find a beautician who can open the shop any earlier."

Bunny huffed and puffed, but dared not press the point. She feared it would appear low-class—something she wanted to avoid. At least Hutch had arranged for a limo to pick her up at the hotel and whisk her off to Gracie Mansion, so she wouldn't have to worry about hailing a cab. He had attended to that last detail before leaving the previous evening. She didn't expect to see him until just before the ceremony, and now she wondered what he had been up to during his last few hours at *liberty*.

Hutch spent his last night as a bachelor at a friend's home on Long Island. He didn't want to tempt superstition by seeing his bride before the ceremony. Besides, he could easily get in nine holes of golf before the wedding.

He considered himself a lucky man to be marrying a member of the English aristocracy. *It might help smooth foreign relations with the British government.* The British were investigating unsafe conditions at his mines in South Africa.

He thought Antonia was attractive and she was certainly sexually spirited, although sometimes she said or did things that were a bit déclassé for a "lady" of her stature.

It didn't worry him, though. If the marriage didn't

work out to his advantage, Antonia would just become another former Mrs. Hutchinson Smythe, along with his three other ex-wives.

CHAPTER TWENTY-NINE

NIGEL FLOATED IN THE CENTER OF A GIANT ORB. IT
reminded him of an iridescent soap bubble. The three
spheres of the Celestial Hierarchy, as well as the human
inhabitants of Heaven and Purgatory and the souls of
ghosts seeking closure for lives ended by unnatural
causes surrounded him.

The Celestials wanted to analyze the seventy-two
hours Nigel had spent with Evangeline. The souls would
be his jury. However, unlike an earthly jury, they would
only provide human opinion to divine emanations that
had *never* been human.

Around him, rings of light spun like a gyroscope,
blinding him at times. The faster the voices spoke, the
faster the rings rotated. And although they didn't make
a sound, the swirling rings created static friction within
the orb that sizzled.

He didn't really have a chance to defend himself. His thoughts were extracted automatically as the disembodied voices dissected his use of high-level paranormal protocol and debated its legality.

The pressure within the orb continued to build until Nigel felt it would surely explode. Then everything went dark.

Bunny arrived at the Mayor's residence just as the clock struck twelve. *Cinderella in reverse,* she thought, as the Mayor's secretary, Margaret Harrington, greeted her.

"Lady Antonia, you look radiant."

Bunny beamed. She had worked hard to look good. It was nice to hear her effort had paid off.

She had expected Gracie Mansion to be much more lavish. Instead, the two-story federal-style building with its wraparound porch reminded her of a boarding house or an inn. Bunny pictured elderly guests sitting in rocking chairs on the veranda sipping Pimm's while talking about the war.

The secretary interrupted her reverie. "We may have a little delay."

Suddenly, Bunny felt her stomach flip-flop. "It's not Hutch, is it? Is he all right? Tell me he's all right."

"Mr. Smythe is just fine. He's with the Mayor in the library having drinks. The other guests are all assembled in the front parlor. Everything is ready to go.

"It's just that we're having trouble confirming your identity through the British Records Office. They say their archives are in a state of disarray, but they're doing their best to validate your information." She gestured toward the doorway. "Right this way."

Bunny felt her whole world crumbling. Why did they need to validate her identity? All right, maybe she wasn't whom she pretended to be, but why should the Americans care?

Mrs. Harrington opened the door to the library. "Lady Southerland is here," she said brightly.

Hutch greeted her warmly, kissing both her cheeks in the European style.

The Mayor took her hand and gallantly lifted it to his lips. "Lady Southerland, may I congratulate you on your impending wedding.

"We still have a few details to iron out. While we're waiting, let me suggest that we start with the luncheon and have the ceremony afterwards. That way, we won't keep our guests waiting. And it will save us from watching every tick of the clock during the time it takes for overseas confirmation to come in.

"May I escort you into lunch? Your groom will have that pleasure for the rest of your lives together, but for now, it would make this humble Mayor happy."

Bunny allowed him to escort her into the dining room. She wanted to sneak away by herself to think, but she would have to wait. First, they forced her to stand by the door in a receiving line to greet the guests. She stood between Hutch and the Mayor, shaking hands for what must have been a solid half-hour. She may have looked radiant when she first arrived, but now her smile no longer reached her eyes and she couldn't wait for the charade to end.

Whatever made her think that she might actually have a shot at *happily ever after*?

Finally, the last hand was shaken and the last

inanity shared. The Mayor led her to her seat at the head of the table, just to his right. Hutch sat on the Mayor's left. Bunny wasn't even going to be allowed to sit next to the man she had thought she was going to marry.

She felt the salt of tears sting her eyes, but fought the urge to cry, knowing it would only add insult to injury. *Nothing looks worse than mascara running down a woman's face.*

She sat silently, totally absorbed in her own dilemma. She only spoke when a direct question was asked and hardly ate a thing. She planned to slip away before word arrived that she was a fraud. But just as she was about to make an excuse to leave the room, servers wheeled in a giant wedding cake and a jazz trio began playing the "Wedding March." Bunny and Hutch were asked to pose with the frothy multi-tiered confection for pictures, before being led back to the table for cake and coffee.

Finally, she saw her chance. "Excuse me, gentlemen," she said after watching everyone enjoy the fruits of her wedding reception. "I really should powder my nose before the ceremony." *More like take a powder,* she thought.

As she stood up, Mrs. Harrington rushed into the room. "Your Honor," she addressed the Mayor, "the cable from England has arrived."

Bunny had a strong fortitude, but it was all too much for her. She fainted into a heap at the Mayor's feet.

EG.

CHAPTER THIRTY

THE PRINCIPALITY TRANSPORTED EVANGELINE TO THE Court of the Dominions. At first, she felt battered by the speed at which her thoughts were ripped from her psyche, but she refused to be cowed. Instead, she forcefully introduced her own ideas about what was going on—into her consciousness.

As they had with Nigel, the rings of lights orbited at a blinding rate of speed. And Evangeline concentrated on making them slow down. As she forced her thoughts to the forefront, the rings lost velocity and finally came to a halt.

Whether the Dominions wanted to or not, Evangeline compelled them to consider her opinion.

A voice literally boomed, "How dare you interfere with the Celestial Hierarchy?"

Evangeline willed her own voice to sound strong.

"I dare to do what's right for the benefit of mankind."

"You know nothing about benefiting mankind. You have seen merely *years* of *man's* contributions and abuses to a single planetary body within a vast, limitless Universe. The Celestial Hierarchy has reigned since time immemorial. Do not talk to us about the benefit of mankind."

Evangeline lowered her head, humbled. "I was trying to save a life."

"Were you saving that life with the purest of intentions, or because you wanted to thwart the person trying to end that life?"

Evangeline trembled. She had not previously paid much attention to how her feelings for Bunny might be guiding her actions, but she knew Nigel had mentioned it, and the Celestial Hierarchy obviously thought it was important, as well. She cringed as the stinging rebuke overpowered her. She had allowed her distaste for Bunny to blind her.

Her arrogance suddenly drained away, leaving her empty. Evangeline's shoulders sagged and tears welled up in her eyes. She had no alternative but to accept the truth. The reasons for her actions were not as pure as she wanted to believe.

"I'm sorry," she whispered. She wasn't a spy anymore. The game had ended. Unconsciously, she surrendered.

The rings started spinning again. Evangeline felt their energy coursing through her veins, until she thought she would not be able to stand it for another second.

Then she felt nothing.

Feuermacht did his best to dress in a way that would blend in. Once again, he donned his brown suit and hat, and eyeglasses that looked like they had been made for a man with extremely poor sight. However, even though the convex lenses looked very thick, their thinner centers were crafted without the curve necessary to correct vision. Feuermacht had 20/20 vision. The spectacles allowed him to see where he was going, yet people only remembered his thick glasses and not his face.

He entered the Waldorf Astoria and approached the front desk. In perfect, unaccented English he said, "I have a delivery here for …" He paused before pulling a piece of paper out of his pocket. "Lady Antonia Southerland."

"Lady Southerland is out. If you'd like to leave it with us, we'll make sure she gets it."

"Thank you." Feuermacht handed over the package, certain the Waldorf Astoria management would take care of the rest.

Bunny and Hutch held hands as they stood together before the Mayor. O'Dwyer smiled at them. "I now pronounce you condemned to death."

"No," Bunny screamed, as someone slapped handcuffs on her wrists.

"Prepare the poison elixir," the Mayor decreed, "and bring it to me."

His secretary arrived a moment later, wearing a gas mask. Hutch and the Mayor also pulled on gas masks, and Mrs. Harrington opened a small glass jar filled with a noxious green liquid. "Lady Antonia, you must inhale this," she ordered. Her voice, muffled by the mask, sounded far away.

Bunny tried to hold her breath, but knew it would only delay the inevitable.

Bunny could feel acrid fumes prickling the inside of her nostrils. She turned her head from side to side to get away from it, but it kept following her. Finally she swatted at it, opening her eyes. Mrs. Harrington held a vial of smelling salts under her nose. Bunny suddenly realized where she was, and the bile rose in her throat.

"Lady Southerland, are you all right?"

Didn't this woman get it? She wasn't Lady Southerland.

"Antonia, dear, what happened?" Hutch bent over her, his face etched with concern.

The Mayor's secretary answered for her. "It's the excitement. And I'll bet she hasn't eaten a thing. No bride would. She would never risk spilling something on her beautiful outfit."

They still think I'm Lady Southerland. They haven't read the cable yet.

"I say we get on with the service before we lose the bride!" The Mayor's remark elicited a few chuckles from the crowd.

"That sounds like a good idea." Hutch helped her up. "Let me have a look at you." He checked her from all angles. "You're still ravishing," he said as he offered her his arm.

Mrs. Harrington shoved the cable in her pocket. "If you want to wait in the Mayor's office, I'll move everyone into the parlor for the ceremony."

Mayor O'Dwyer escorted Bunny and Hutch into his office. Bunny sat down in a club chair, while the Mayor and Hutch discussed their preference for hand rolled Cuban cigars.

Finally, the secretary returned to stay with Bunny while the Mayor and Hutch took their places in the parlor. A chamber music ensemble began playing the "Bridal Chorus" from *Lohengrin*. Mrs. Harrington literally pulled Bunny out of the chair she rested in, and pushed her out the door and down the aisle.

Hutch walked up to meet Bunny and escorted her the rest of the way, with his arm snaked firmly around her waist. The Mayor's secretary walked around to the front of the room and handed O'Dwyer a book containing the service.

The Mayor's ceremony was not as short as Bunny had hoped, but she listened attentively while he spoke, wondering when the bubble would burst.

She could see Mrs. Harrington standing to her right and tried not to look at her, but she couldn't help staring when the secretary retrieved the cable from her pocket and began reading it.

As the Mayor said, "If anyone present can show just cause as to why this couple may not be legally joined together," Mrs. Harrington made eye contact with Bunny.

Bunny froze as the Mayor continued. "You should now declare it, or hereafter hold your peace."

CHAPTER THIRTY-ONE

W HEN SHE OPENED HER EYES, EVANGELINE FOUND
herself in the Presidential Suite of the Waldorf Astoria.

"Glad to have you back, Evie. It was touch and go
for a while."

"Oh, Nigel." Evangeline threw her arms around
him and hugged him tightly. "I thought I'd never see
you again and that I would be the one responsible for
damning you to hell. I'm so glad you're here."

"We're both here, Evie, and our trials with the
Dominions have had some pretty good consequences."

"What do you mean?"

"The *Collective* was impressed, first by your
tenacious spirit and then by your humility when you
realized you may be irrationally trying to punish Bunny.
So they allowed you to come back to find your murderer,
that way you can rest in peace."

"So we're back where we started."

"Not really. I already know, through you, who my murderer is. I've just got to bring Bunny to justice. But that's my mission, not yours."

"You still need to identify your murderer," he continued. "And the *Collective* has agreed to allow you to learn some special psychic skills, like telekinesis, so you don't have to depend on me. You'll be better equipped to handle tricky situations, including emergencies. Of course, if you get into trouble, it will be solely your own undoing."

"How comforting."

"They want you to take responsibility for your actions, Evie."

"I will, Nigel. But the Celestial Hierarchy and the *Collective* are very intimidating. They can read our minds and look into our hearts. Sometimes, I'm afraid to think."

"The Celestial Hierarchy is only interested in what we're thinking when we're brought before the Dominions. And the *Collective* isn't a *they*. It's a *we*. You and I are part of the *Collective*. Anyway, I'm sure you'll rise to the occasion. Just embrace the *Collective* instead of trying to shield your intentions.

"I think it time to start applying your talents as a spy to determine who may have killed you. And yes, I concede that it may have been Bunny or Feuermacht, but I think it's more likely that it's someone else. Let's start with Bruchman."

Evangeline unconsciously shook her head from side to side as she thought back to her last day of life. "I don't see how it could have been him, Nigel. It's true that I was preparing to testify against him, as well as other highly placed Nazi officers, during the war trials. But Bruchman was in jail at the time."

"That doesn't mean he couldn't have ordered your death."

"You think he hired an assassin from behind bars?"

"It's possible."

"Wouldn't it be more likely that someone not yet behind bars, might have been implicated by my testimony?"

"That's another possibility. Do you want to start there?"

"I wouldn't know how. I believe all of the people Colin and I identified as criminals were arrested and awaiting trial. I don't recall anyone on our preliminary list who was still at large."

"Which is why it may be better to start with Bruchman. He was the first man you were scheduled to testify against. What do you know about him?"

"Not much." She paused. "But didn't the *Collective* tell you that he had a lover in the Reichstag?"

"Do you think his lover may have tried to kill you?"

"I don't even know who she is. It would take a lot of sleuthing to get her name."

"Let me think about that, Evie. I don't think we should go to Saint Peter right now and ask for a favor. But we can ask the *Collective* if *they* know something about her. For now, let's get back to Bunny and Hutch. They weren't here when I arrived and I don't know where they've gone."

***

Washington, D.C. had been blessed with the kind of day when most people forget their problems and act like they don't have a care in the world. But the Secret Service agents who had accompanied President Truman to New York would not get to enjoy the magnificent weather. Instead, they were called on the carpet for allowing someone to sabotage the President's car.

It didn't matter that they discovered the problem before the President was put at risk. What did matter was that someone had tampered with the vehicle, and Frank Wilson needed to identify that person.

Wilson had been the head of the Secret Service since 1937. His claim to fame—insisting that someone write down the serial numbers on the money used to pay the ransom for Charles Lindbergh's baby—eventually led to the arrest and conviction of Bruno Richard Hauptmann for the child's abduction and murder.

The Lindbergh kidnapping had been dubbed the crime of the century. Wilson didn't need another major crime, like the assassination of a President, disturbing his peace. He had scheduled an informal hearing in his office that afternoon. It involved all the agents who had accompanied the President on the *Ferdinand Magellan*, and Wilson was sure they were all sweating bullets. With any kind of luck, he'd get to the bottom of the sabotage before day's end.

Back at Gracie Mansion, the Mayor asked Hutch if he agreed to take Lady Antonia Southerland for "richer or poorer."

Bunny barely heard his answer. The words sounded indistinct and far away. Everything around

Bunny seemed to have slowed down dramatically. In contrast, she could hear her own heart beating loudly, inside her head—like her own personal death knell. She thought she heard Hutch say "I do," but she wasn't sure. She stopped staring at Mrs. Harrington and turned her attention to Hutch. He looked back at her, smiling.

Over his shoulder, Bunny could still see Mrs. Harrington holding the cable.

The Mayor forged ahead. "Do you, Lady Antonia Southerland, take this man, Hutchinson Reginald Smythe, to be your lawful wedded husband, to have and to hold from this day forward, for better, for worse, for richer, for poorer, in sickness and in health, to love, cherish, and obey, till death do you part?"

Bunny thought the Mayor might be talking to her and forced herself to look away from Mrs. Harrington. "Pardon?"

Hutch and O'Dwyer stared at her for a second before the Mayor repeated the vows. Bunny looked at Mrs. Harrington. The woman smiled.

"I do," Bunny croaked.

The Mayor sighed in relief. "Then, by the power vested in me by the state of New York, I now pronounce you man and wife."

Time for a wardrobe change. Feuermacht returned to his room, put on a dark gray suit with an ascot, and glued a fake handlebar mustache above his upper lip. He slipped on black shoes and a black bowler hat. The last piece of his new *costume* was a gold pince-nez.

He headed back to the Waldorf Astoria, stopping along the way to buy the afternoon paper.

At the hotel, he sat on an upholstered chair opposite the reception desk and pretended to read. He wanted to be nearby when the staff presented Bunny with her special box of candies.

CHAPTER THIRTY-TWO

Lady Antonia Southerland Smythe swept through the doors of the Waldorf Astoria as if she owned the hotel. Her attitude had completely changed— from nearly defeated to utterly conceited. She struck an imperious pose. She was a millionaire's wife and she expected to be treated like one.

Hutch stopped at the front desk and asked if there were any messages.

"No messages, sir, but we do have a parcel for Lady Antonia. It was delivered this morning."

Hutch looked at the wrappings and lifted the package to his nose, sniffing it. He turned to his new wife. "Sweets for the sweet, dearest. Someone has sent chocolates to celebrate our big day, no doubt." He winked at her. "And I'm quite familiar with this candy shop. They make the best bonbons in town."

He handed Bunny the parcel and took her elbow. "We've got just enough time to pack before our train leaves for Washington."

"You're going out of town?" The hotel manager's face registered surprise. "Would you like us to hold your suite, or will you be away for an extended period?"

"We'll only be gone a few days," Hutch answered. "Lady Antonia has expressed an interest in seeing Washington and I have some business down there, so we've decided to mix business with pleasure. But we'll only be packing a few things. We're leaving everything else in the suite, and I'd appreciate it if you would hold it for us."

"Of course, sir." The manager knew how to appease a *very good* guest. Besides, if a European dignitary or an Arabian prince showed up, the Waldorf Astoria would do what it always did when the Presidential Suite was already in use: find alternative rooms for its guest to stay in, just like it did for President Truman.

"They're going to Washington?" Evangeline unconsciously slapped Nigel's arm with the back of her hand. "It looks like *everyone* is going to Washington. I'd bet my life the President is still in danger."

"You wouldn't have much of a bet there, Evie." Nigel pointed out.

"My reputation, then," she answered.

"And I'll bet you're right. We should probably hop the train with them, just like we did with the President on the *Ferdinand Magellan*."

"What about the Dominions? How do you know this is something they'd want us to do?"

"Because I can feel it. If the *Collective* agrees there's an unwarranted threat, we'll be allowed to board with Bunny and Hutch and follow them to Union Station."

"How will we know?" She sighed. "We need some kind of sign."

Siegfried Feuermacht suddenly stood up—and stared right through Evie at the departing Smythes.

"Is that Feuermacht?"

Nigel laughed. "If that isn't a sign, I don't know what is."

"Should we follow him?"

"I think we should stick with Bunny and Hutch on their trip to Washington. If Feuermacht's part of the plot, he'll inevitably end up there, as well."

Feuermacht returned to his hotel to pack. He planned to catch a bus to Jersey City, where he would board the B&O National Limited. He wondered if Bunny and Hutch would be on the same train. It wasn't scheduled to leave for a couple of hours, which was good, because he had something to do first.

Feuermacht needed to get rid of the items he used to *doctor* Bunny's candy. He couldn't dump everything en masse. It would look too suspicious and could be incriminating. Instead, he packed them in a paper bag and walked to Rockefeller Center. Every couple of blocks or so, he dumped another item in a trash container. The long walk gave him plenty of opportunities to dispose of almost everything. He'd dump the last few pieces in Washington.

On the bus, he placed his suitcase on the seat next to him to prevent uninvited guests from getting too close.

The ride was uneventful and tedious. He didn't find the landscape very appealing, and the number of stops that the bus made during the trip irritated him.

The Jersey City Station didn't particularly impress Feuermacht, but the *National Limited* more than made up for it. The train was modern, stylish, and full-service, offering passengers dining cars, sleeping compartments, and shower stalls. Its sleek appearance and luxurious touches reminded him of something that could have been engineered in his homeland.

The ticket agent boasted the train even had a manicurist and a barber onboard. "Just in case you want to shave off that beard of yours, *Mr. Jones*." Little did the agent know that spirit gum remover would do a better job of that than any straight razor.

Millicent Forsythe loved to entertain the high and the mighty of Washington, D.C.

She might not be the *hostess with the mostest*—that designation was reserved for Perle Mesta—but Millicent easily held her own when opening her doors to government leaders and other Washington officials. And she had the perfect home for entertaining them—Le Havre House.

The French-style residence with its mansard roof and neo-baroque interior had fifty-two rooms, including an impressive three-story entrance hall with a balcony decorated with ornately carved panels.

She could entertain hundreds of guests at a time, and they were always appropriately impressed with her priceless art collection and ornate chandeliers.

That afternoon, she surrounded herself with a

cadre of caterers and decorators. She made lists, and they made haste, readying the house for an elaborate dinner in honor of the President of the United States. Every elected official, lobbyist, and political insider in Washington tried to get an invitation, but Millicent controlled the guest list with an iron fist. The only last-minute change she allowed was the addition of millionaire-industrialist Hutchinson Smythe.

Her husband had called her to say Smythe and his new wife were traveling to D.C. and wanted to have dinner with the Forsythes. She impetuously told him to invite them to the party. Smythe was rich and handsome. Besides, she wanted to meet his latest *mistake*.

Frank Wilson grilled each member of the President's security team. He had a stenographer take down every word so he could cross-reference individual details until he had a complete picture of what had transpired onboard the *Ferdinand Magellan* on the day the President's car was sabotaged. He was down to his last interview and still didn't understand where a breakdown in command might have occurred.

John Cullen entered the room and solemnly greeted his boss. John was Wilson's most trusted agent, but Cullen had filed his request to retire at the end of the year. Wilson suspected that men at the end of their tenure sometimes let their guard down. He knew if he grilled Cullen the man would only answer the direct question in as few words as possible. However, if he approached Cullen in a conversational way, John might feel comfortable enough to give Wilson information the chief might not otherwise be able to pry out of him.

In the end, what he learned from Cullen turned out to be the last thing he expected.

EG.

CHAPTER THIRTY-THREE

"This is it?" Bunny expressed surprised at the size of the Pullman drawing room onboard the *National Limited*. She had expected something more extravagant than the compact room she stood in.

"What did you expect, dearest?" Hutch laughed. "An entire train car like the President has? I think that's a bit over the top—even for me."

"It's just that this is so … small."

"You women. You're always so concerned with size." He winked at his new bride.

Bunny smiled. "Mr. Smythe, I'm sure I don't know what you mean."

Hutch slipped his arms around his wife's waist saying, "I think you know exactly what I'm talking about," before kissing her.

***

"You see, sir, I thought I heard someone entering the train from the opposite end, and when I turned, my pen …" John Cullen paused.

"Go on. Your pen …"

John looked Frank Wilson directly in the eye. "My pen was suspended in midair, with nothing supporting it. I just stared at it for a second. I couldn't believe it was real. But then I felt in my pocket and my new Inkograph was gone. Then …" John paused again.

"Then what?" Frank asked, surprised at the direction the conversation had taken.

"Then it dropped to about a foot off the ground, changed direction, and propelled sideways under the Lincoln."

"What do you think would make it do that?"

"I don't know, sir. It was like it had a mind of its own. Then Stephens came in, so I left with him to brief the others about our arrival. But I went back later, sir, to see if there were any air leaks that could have caused an updraft. I looked for tripwires. Nylon filament. I found nothing.

"The big shock came when I looked under the car for my pen. That's when I noticed four flat tires and the broken brake line. Our forensic crime laboratory says they found a pinhole in the line, but couldn't say if it's related. Talk about overkill.

"I ordered everyone onboard into the parlor car, excluding the President, of course, and started inquiries into who was where at what times." He opened a briefcase and took out a pad. "That information is all here." He handed it to Frank.

"Have you formulated a conclusion, then?"

"No. I handpicked the security detail. I'd trust those men with my life. The train crew members were all regulars. No new personnel there. And the wait staff came directly from the White House. They're part of the President's personal staff.

"The train was contained," John continued, "so logic dictates that it couldn't have happened onboard the *Ferdinand Magellan*. Yet those tires weren't flat when the car was loaded.

"It's possible someone tampered with the car on Track 61. That area's pretty remote, but it's not sealed. Someone intent on harming the president could have accessed the siding through the tunnels."

"Are you suggesting the tires had small punctures like the brake line" Frank asked, "to cause a slow leak?"

"That's what I was hoping for, but according to forensics, there are no punctures in any of the tires. They say there's no earthly reason for them to all go flat on their own."

"Well, this is cozy." Evangeline looked around Bunny and Hutch's drawing room with an eye for efficiency.

"Look, Nigel," she continued, "this must convert into a bed, and there's another one on the other side. And that"—she pointed above the window—"is probably another berth."

She poked her head through a narrow door. "Did you see this tiny commode?"

"Yes. It's all very nicely laid out. But I bet a few days cooped up in one of these would make a traveler go stir-crazy."

"Nonsense, Nigel. It has all the comforts of home."

"Really? Is there a bathtub up on the roof?"

"Planning a little good-natured voyeurism?"

"You said *all* the comforts of home."

"They don't need that many comforts. We'll be in Washington, D.C., by tomorrow. I only hope we'll learn something useful in time to save the President's life."

"Just remember, Evie, this isn't about you and Bunny. It's about protecting Harry S. Truman."

"That's all I care about, Nigel. Honestly."

"Then let's make ourselves useful. It's time to inspect all the sleeping compartments, roomettes, and drawing rooms to see if our good friend Siegfried Feuermacht is onboard."

"What are we going to do about him if we find him?"

"I don't know, Evie. I guess it depends on why he's on this train."

Millicent Forsythe looked at the American-flag decorations with disdain. "You want to hang those red, white and blue buntings over *my* French-silk window valences? Whatever for?"

"You said this party is in honor of the President."

"This isn't a political event. It's a social event with a prominent political guest. Take those silly things away." She flicked her hand through the air, in dismissal.

"Well, Mrs. Forsythe, how would you suggest I decorate the room?"

"This room is already well-decorated. You're only here to embellish it. It's fall. The season is changing. Surely you can find something in that theme that you can use to *enhance* this room without turning it into a garish mess."

"Let me see what I can do." In his hurry to leave, the chastened decorator nearly collided with the butler, who entered the ballroom to summon his employer.

"Mrs. Forsythe, we have a problem in the kitchen."

Millicent's attention was immediately diverted to a new dilemma concerning her party. She would never admit it, but she believed conquering the small challenges of putting a really good dinner party together was half the fun.

Like the Smythes, Feuermacht had also reserved a drawing room on the *National Limited*. He could walk to the dining car or observation dome if he wanted to spy on his fellow passengers. And because he had a private toilet, he could adopt several different disguises without attracting attention.

He knew Bunny would want to have a late dinner, so he planned to go to the dining car around nine. That way he would be in place by the time Bunny and Hutch arrived. His chance to see the "honeymooners" at any other time during the trip was probably nil, but he didn't really care about what they were up to. He just wanted to know they were on the train.

It might even be fun to torment Bunny. Maybe he would let her recognize him. That would put the fear of God into her. He just had to be careful that no one else could identify him.

Feuermacht smiled. The idea of annoying Bunny made him feel warm all over. Of course, the possibility existed that she might not show up if she had indulged herself with some of his special bonbons. He'd just have to wait and see.

EG

CHAPTER THIRTY-FOUR

WHEN EVANGELINE AND NIGEL FINALLY DISCOVERED Feuermacht's compartment, they found him in front of a mirror gluing a full white beard to his face. It would complement his newly powdered hair. He had switched the part in his hair from the right side to the left, and the change made him look like a much older man.

Evangeline studied him. If she hadn't arrived in time to witness him attaching the fake beard, she might not have recognized him. But now, as she stared into his pale blue eyes, she knew for sure that Sebastian Faust was a cover for Siegfried Feuermacht.

Feuermacht stopped and looked over his shoulder, as if he sensed Evangeline and Nigel's presence. After a moment, he continued his artistry.

The couple watched as Feuermacht trimmed his fake beard, then used tweezers and glue to stick the trimmed hairs to his eyebrows, changing their shape and appearance.

Evangeline's jaw dropped when he used a fine brush to paint thin lines of rubber cement around his eyes and pinched his skin together to form wrinkles.

She was so mesmerized by the transformation that she did not bother to turn away when he removed his clothing to change into a worn, oversized suit. He cinched the pants with an old belt, to make it look like he had suffered a recent reversal of fortune and had lost a great deal of weight.

"He's going to an awful lot of trouble for a man who's just taking a train to Washington," Evangeline noted.

"He's probably afraid Bunny will ID him and the American police will hand him over to Interpol," Nigel reasoned.

"Are you defending him?" she asked in astonishment.

"No, Evie. I'm just saying he's wearing a disguise so no one will recognize him. I'm sure there are a lot of people, besides yourself, who would love to get their hands on Feuermacht, and not because they want to be his friend."

"I think you should stick to Feuermacht and I'll stick to Bunny, and we'll see if they meet up."

"Considering the only places to go on this train are the dining car and the bar in the observation car, we can be pretty certain they'll eventually run into each other."

"Yes. But it's how they react when they meet that will be the telling point."

Feuermacht put away his scissors and glue and donned a pair of wire-rimmed glasses. Then he grabbed a sturdy cane and put his ear to the door for a few seconds before finally pulling it open and hobbling down the corridor toward the dining car.

Frank Wilson didn't know what to make of John Cullen's statements. He had cross-referenced John's notes with the statements the other agents had given him and everything checked out. Interestingly, John's partner had stated that when he found John in the boxcar, the older agent looked like he had 'just seen a ghost.'

He thought about John's description of his pen dangling in midair. He wondered if one of the other agents had played a practical joke. He didn't want to think his men fooled around on the job, but it was a much better explanation than citing anything *supernatural*.

Wilson rewrote his report, leaving out any mention of John looking like he had seen a ghost. That was something the administration did not need to know. If J. Edgar Hoover ever caught wind of the ghost reference, he would probably try to use it to wrest control of the Secret Service away from the Treasury Department, so it could be placed under the jurisdiction of the Federal Bureau of Investigation. Wilson hated the thought. *Not under my watch.*

It was late, but Wilson took the time to drive out to the siding where the *Ferdinand Magellan* was berthed when not in use. He wanted to examine the inside of the boxcar with his own eyes.

Millicent Forsythe took a deep breath. Her favorite

chef had prepared many of the items she would be serving at the reception for President Truman, and everything tasted so good, she sampled them all twice. There were traditional dishes that she knew Truman favored, like filet mignon with mushroom sauce, asparagus hollandaise, and hearts of lettuce with Roquefort dressing. But she had also chosen some of her own tried-and-true favorites, like celery stuffed with crabmeat, oyster soup, and fresh lobster with drawn butter.

She originally planned to serve only strawberries sabayon as the final course. But in the end, she caved in and added chocolate brownies and ice cream to the dessert menu, knowing the President enjoyed them.

Of course, she had to be sure she selected the right wines to accompany the various dishes, so she sampled those, as well. Now, she felt a bit bloated and wished she had entrusted the *tasting* chores to her butler. At least she was confident her guests wouldn't go hungry.

Hutch waited patiently as Bunny dressed for dinner. She had changed her outfit twice before finally slipping back into the first dress she had tried on. He would never have guessed that selecting the *right* jewelry would be as difficult, but was pleased when she put on the earrings he had given her as a gift. Finally, she announced she was ready to dine.

He took her arm and together they tentatively made their way to the dining car, barely noticing the scenery as the train hurtled across the Mid-Atlantic States. Bunny complained every time they had to exit and enter another car, and Hutch sighed in relief when his bride finally arrived at the dining car, unscathed.

As the porter showed them to a table, an elderly man dropped his eyeglasses in the aisle. Hutch stepped around Bunny and bent over to pick them up, but when he turned back to his wife, he found the old man's spectacles weren't the only thing that hit the floor.

Bunny had fainted, causing a spectacle of a different sort.

This is really getting to be tiresome. If Hutch had known his new wife swooned at the drop of a hat, or a pair of eyeglasses, he probably would not have married her.

CHAPTER THIRTY-FIVE

A PORTER HELPED HUTCH LIFT HIS WIFE AND CARRY HER to a secluded corner booth. They moved clumsily, and brushed against more than one table, pulling tablecloths askew and irritating diners who grabbed onto their wine glasses to keep them from falling. The diners weren't all successful. Their annoyed stares irritated Hutch, but there was nothing he could do about it.

"We could use a glass of water here," a rotund man said to the porter. He held out his hand to Hutch. "Dr. Joseph Shields. It looks like you could use my assistance."

"This is the second time today she's passed out like this." Hutch's tone sounded more frustrated than concerned.

"Is there any underlying reason you can think of that would make her faint? Has she been sick lately? Has it been a while since she's eaten? Anything like that?"

"Not that I know of, although she only picked at her food today at lunch. But everyone said that's because we were getting married."

"Congratulations. When's the big day?"

"Today. Like I said, she only picked at her food, and then she fainted just before the ceremony."

"Well, that certainly could do it."

"But now it's happening again," Hutch groaned. "Why?"

"It could be wedding-night jitters."

"Oh, it's not that, the lady and I have … Well … It's not that."

"I see," the doctor replied. "Is it possible …" He paused. "Could she be with child?"

Hutch blanched. "I don't know. Do you think she could be?"

"She would need a thorough examination to determine that. But considering what you just hinted at, it sounds like a possibility."

"A baby," Hutch moaned.

"You did say you're married."

"Yes. But I hadn't really considered starting a family this soon."

"You may *have* to consider it. Are you getting off in Baltimore?"

"No, we're going on to Washington."

"I know of a good doctor in the Georgetown area. Here's his name." The doctor took out a calling card and wrote on the back of it. "Look him up when you get there. He'll be able to give you a definitive answer."

The porter returned with a glass of water. The doctor flicked a few drops of it on Bunny's face and she pulled away. "She'll be okay. But take her to the doctor. If she's pregnant, the sooner you know about it, the better."

"Thank you." Hutch shook the doctor's hand.

When he turned to Bunny, her eyelids were fluttering open.

Pregnant. That's the last thing Hutch wanted. Children meant child support when the marriage foundered, and it was starting to look like this one wouldn't last long. Who needed a wife who fainted for the smallest reason? Even worse, who needed a wife who tired herself out attending to a child instead of him?

Oh well, it didn't matter. His lawyers would know exactly how to take care of the problem.

Evangeline and Nigel lingered in a nearby booth in the dining car. "Could you imagine Bunny as somebody's mother?" she mused.

"I don't know, Evie. She may be pregnant, but I doubt it highly, considering she fainted right in front our favorite villain."

"I really find it infuriating, Nigel, that you always say something logical just when the topic gets juicy. Next time, would you humor me by agreeing with me, or by saying something completely frivolous and witty, just to give our mission the *illusion* of sophisticated fun?"

"I guess I really *have* changed since I died. There were times when I would have instinctively reacted the way you're asking me to react. But now, with the Dominions watching over our shoulders, I guess I've become a stickler for doing the right thing."

"And I always feel guilty because it seems like I'm trying to lead you astray. I used to be the logical one,

Nigel. Now, I feel like we've exchanged personas."

"Maybe, if we work at it, we can meet in the middle, Evie. I'll try to loosen up. But you have to be a little more serious about what's allowed by the *Collective*."

Evangeline shook her head and gave Nigel a wry smile. "Who knew death would be so complicated?"

Millicent Forsythe tightly controlled every aspect of her party, but there was one thing she couldn't control: her husband.

Gregory Forsythe's only purpose in life was to please himself, even if it meant sneaking his mistress into the many parties hosted by his wife. His womanizing always got him into trouble, and if he didn't hold the keys to the family fortune, he'd probably be in dire straits. There were always stories circulating about Gregory and they were seldom flattering. To make matters worse, everyone knew him as a dyed-in-the-wool Republican— the polar opposite of his wife's guest of honor, President Harry S. Truman.

Gregory could best be described as a loose cannon, poised to shoot a gaping hole through what Millicent hoped would be *the* major event of the season.

A lone security guard watched over the *Ferdinand Magellan*. The train had been sealed shut—the guard posted only to make sure no one tried anything devious, like sabotaging it.

Frank Wilson flashed his ID and told the guard to unlock the train. He turned on one of the lanterns inside the dark vehicle and looked from one end of the boxcar to the other. The President's Lincoln had been taken by flatbed truck to a service area, where it was being repaired. Without the vehicle taking up floor space, the boxcar seemed enormous.

Wilson instinctively knew exactly where the Lincoln had been parked. There were a few drops of telltale engine fluids staining the floorboards, and wheel chocks sitting nearby.

As he walked down the length of the car, he lit every lantern to chase the gloom away. Then he did many of the same things John Cullen had done. He looked for unexpected vents or openings where breezes might enter the car. He looked for tripwires. He even got down on his hands and knees to search for anything unusual.

He looked once. He looked twice. He looked three times. But every time his findings were the same. He found no anomalies to explain why four tires would go flat all at once, or why a pen would float in midair and then follow an unusual trajectory on its way to the floor.

Feuermacht sighed contentedly. He had seen the look in Bunny's eyes just before she fainted. She had recognized him and was scared.

She should be scared. He didn't even have to do anything more. She already had possession of the candy, and that would surely do the job for him. Had she already had a piece? Could that be why she fainted? *No,* he chided himself. It had to be pure fear that had sent her crashing to the floor. She had walked in under her own steam and hadn't looked any the worse for wear.

He took a sip of wine and silently toasted himself. The only thing that could have been more perfect would have been the porter seating Bunny and Hutch at his table. He imagined her squirming as she sat across from him, unable to explain herself. The idea made him laugh out loud.

"Something funny, Mr. Jones?" Feuermacht had been seated with a couple from Ontario who were traveling to Saint Louis to see their new grandson.

Feuermacht nodded to the couple. "I was just thinking about the joy you'll feel seeing your grandchild for the first time, and it filled me with happiness."

The wife smiled. "Oh, Mr. Jones, if only you weren't getting off in Washington, you could meet our pride and joy, too."

"I'm sorry I won't be able to do that," Feuermacht said. "But allow me to toast the addition to your family." And he raised the goblet to his lips and savored the wine within.

EG

CHAPTER THIRTY-SIX

UNDER PICTURE-PERFECT OCTOBER SKIES, LANDSCAPERS on the grounds of Le Havre House pruned the hedges and mowed the grass in preparation for Millicent's party. It wouldn't do for the President to twist his ankle on an errant twig. Or for the First Lady to ruin her shoes while walking across an unkempt lawn.

A breeze carried the sweet scent of freshly mown grass through the open French doors, as Millicent admired her decorator's handiwork. The ballroom glistened like a jewel. Her designer may have gotten off to a slow start, but proved his worth in the end.

He had positioned round tables of differing sizes around the perimeter of the ballroom, each draped in floor-length gold lamé, covered by a layer of gauzy tulle. In the center of each table sat a large bowl filled with branches encrusted with gemstones the colors of autumn. Crystal leaves dangled at the end of each tapering bough, and with the sunlight shining through them, they projected red, orange, and gold accents onto the mossy green walls.

Hundreds of identical leaves dangled from the chandeliers and glimmered against the vivid blue silk that sheathed the ceiling, emulating the autumn sky.

The dining room was decorated in a similar fashion. Millicent liked what she saw and instinctively knew the dinner would be a great success.

Now, she only had to decide whether to ignore her husband's antics, or hire someone to follow him around and make sure he toed the line.

Union Station bustled with activity. The Beaux-Arts depot, known as the "Gateway to the Capital," was the only railroad station in America with its own Presidential Suite. Hundreds of people kept the various businesses inside the facility up and running, making the station pulsate like a living entity with a life of its own.

Bunny clutched Hutch's arm as they left the *National Limited*. She hadn't seen Siegfried Feuermacht all morning. Still, she subconsciously needed Hutch to shield her from Feuermacht's evil mechanizations.

Hutch seemed distant and distracted. He'd hardly said two words to her since breakfast. He had actually seemed angry when she had balked at eating in the dining room. He curtly replied, "Suit yourself," and left for breakfast without her.

At first she cried, but then the *old* Bunny mentality kicked in, and she started planning what she could do to make her new husband see things *her way*.

To his credit, Hutch brought back a pastry and a container of coffee for his wife. She cooed over his display of thoughtfulness, while silently cursing him for not producing something more extravagant to soothe her hurt feelings.

Once outside, Hutch hailed a taxicab and they were soon on their way to the heart of the nation.

"Antonia, did you bring a gown with you?"

"Yes, darling. Just in case we decided to go someplace special to celebrate our honeymoon, I wanted to be prepared."

"Good. We're attending the Forsythe party at Le Havre House tonight. It should be quite a bash. I hear the President will be there. Humph. Fancy the wolf in Democrat's clothing blundering into the Republican lair. It should be quite interesting. I'm sure you'll learn a lot about American politics there."

Great. Just what she needed—a lesson in politics. Bunny didn't know whether to laugh or cry. She was excited about attending an important event as Mrs. Hutchinson Smythe, but knew she'd be bored. And she feared someone might be there who could spill the beans about her, publicly identifying her as a fraud.

"I have some business to attend to today," Hutch continued, "so you'll have all afternoon to rest before the big event."

"I had plenty of time to rest on the train. I think I'll do a little shopping."

"That can wait until tomorrow."

"Don't worry, darling. I'll be ready and waiting when you return."

Twenty minutes later they were in their suite at

the Hay-Adams Hotel. As soon as the bellboy put down their bags, Hutch kissed his wife goodbye and took off. Bunny was stunned. She thought they'd spend at least a little time together before Hutch wandered off to take care of business.

Undeterred, she went down to the hotel dining room. She had eaten very little the previous day and had only eaten half the dry pastry Hutch had brought her on the train. She was famished, so when the restaurant hesitated in seating an unescorted woman, she gave them a piece of her mind and trotted out her credentials as Mrs. Hutchinson Smythe—the former Lady Antonia Southerland.

She soon dipped her spoon into a bowl of creamy vichyssoise and her fork into a generous helping of chicken-and-pecan salad, and not until she scraped the bottom of a bowl of blueberry cobbler, did she finally feel sated.

Two women sitting nearby commented on the amount of food Bunny consumed, speculating that she must be eating for *two*.

Gloves covered the buyer's hands, but the clerk in the chemist's shop didn't think it unusual. He had seen other customers do the exact same thing when they bought remedies for a fungal infection. And they all purchased the same product: potassium permanganate. It was well-known that the purple powder helped relieve dermatitis as well as fungus on hands and feet. Hardly anyone ever considered that it could also be used to make explosives.

The customer paid in cash, and then walked to a small grocery store, where he purchased a rolling pin, sugar, and soap. He moved on to a stationery store for cellophane tape, and the plumbing department of a hardware store for a piece of pipe—just another Washingtonian making a few simple purchases for home, or so it seemed.

Frank Wilson had only been to the Oval Office twice before and, oddly enough, his visits had been to two different Oval Offices. The first one had been located in the center of the West Wing of the White House, a windowless interior space that had been destroyed in a fire. He had been there because of the role he played in Al Capone's arrest for income-tax evasion. Several years later, when he was appointed chief of the Secret Service, Wilson was again called into the Oval Office. By then, the office had relocated to the southeast corner of the West Wing, with a door to the Rose Garden and several windows connecting the space to the outside world. It hadn't changed much since then.

Wilson's department may have been entrusted with protecting the President's life, but that didn't mean he felt at ease when called in for a one-on-one meeting at the White House. His discomfort felt especially acute since he didn't have plausible answers for many of the questions he knew the President would ask.

He jumped to his feet when Truman entered the room.

"How are you, Frank?"

"Fine, sir."

"And your wife, Judith?"

"She's fine, sir. Thanks for asking." Wilson smiled. "She'll be pleased to hear you asked about her."

"She's a fine woman."

"I agree, sir."

"So tell me, Frank, what have you found out about my Lincoln?"

Wilson thought back to something John Cullen had said. "Poltergeists, sir."

"Excuse me?"

"Mr. President, my men and I have been over that car with a fine-tooth comb. They didn't find anything out of the ordinary. I didn't find anything, either. I had forensics give it one last sweep first thing this morning, but they couldn't find a splinter of evidence.

"We know the Lincoln was in perfect shape when it arrived in Manhattan. I checked with our office in New York, who investigated the siding at Track 61, and they say there's insufficient evidence to suggest foul play. The only thing that warrants further investigation is a footprint found in one of the tunnels leading to the siding. It could have been made by anyone—a bum looking for a place to sleep, a maintenance man, even one of our own advance team. We're checking that out now."

"What about the agents on duty that night? What do they have to say about the incident?"

Wilson hesitated. "One man reported something odd, but it's so unusual, I can't see how it could possibly be true, so I hate to bring it up."

"Well, if you didn't think you had my full attention before, Frank, you can be sure you have it now. Tell me what he said."

Wilson knew he had painted himself into a corner. "He said he saw his pen hovering in midair before projecting itself under your car."

"What?"

"I know how it sounds, but he's one of our best."

"And …"

"We checked out his story, but there's nothing to support what he says."

"Sounds like the work of the *Invisible Man*."

"Let's hope it's not. If invisibility is anything more than science fiction, we'll have a hell of a job protecting you and the Vice President."

"I'd like to speak to the man whose pen … went astray."

"Yes, sir. I'll call him immediately."

Evangeline and Nigel found Feuermacht in a Washington hotel room. During the war, the Tabard Inn had been used to house women enlisted in the U.S. Navy, but it had returned to serving civilians, and the German had taken a suite there.

Every few minutes, Nigel popped into the bathroom to see what was taking Feuermacht so long. "Didn't this guy ever hear of taking a quick shower? He's soaking in the bathtub."

"I think you're more fixated on him than I am on Bunny."

"I'll admit the man intrigues me."

"And he may be trying to kill the President."

Nigel agreed. "I doubt he's here to see the sights."

Evangeline played devil's advocate. "Maybe he's just trying to scare Bunny to death?"

"Then I'd say he's doing a pretty good job. He's already frightened her enough to make her faint. If he can surprise her when Hutch, or anyone else for that matter, isn't around, he may succeed in killing her."

"I think he's having too much fun tormenting her. If he kills her, he'll have no one left to play with."

Twenty minutes later Feuermacht emerged from the bathroom sporting a handlebar mustache. He had on a suit that made him look much heavier than his true size and a bowler hat. He pulled a few items out of his suitcase and stuffed them into his pocket.

"Interesting." Nigel commented. "I wonder what he's got under there?"

Feuermacht headed out the door, and Evangeline and Nigel followed him onto a streetcar en route to Cleveland Park.

When Feuermacht reached his destination, he casually strolled around the area, studying the lay of the land. He stopped at one immense home and knocked on the front door, asking for directions. A butler answered his questions.

"Thank you, Mr. … what did you say your name was?"

"I didn't."

"I feel that I can't properly thank you without knowing your name."

"It's Phillips."

"Thank you, Mr. Phillips. You have been most kind."

Feuermacht walked down the long driveway toward the street before circling around to the back of the house. He watched as a catering crew unloaded a delivery truck. Some of the men were dressed in street clothes, but others wore black jackets with white shirts and bow ties, which is what Feuermacht had been betting on.

He ducked behind some bushes and removed his outer garments and mustache. Underneath, he wore clothing, similar to what the wait staff had on. He had *borrowed* it from one of the National Limited dining-car waiters while the man slept.

Feuermacht rummaged around in his jacket pocket, pulling out a bow tie and heavy black-rimmed glasses before approaching the back of the house.

"Who are you?" one of the waiters asked in a heavy Italian accent.

"Mr. Phillips, the butler, hired me. He told me you might need help tonight. He said it's an important party and he wants to make sure there are enough people to care for all the guests."

Another worker emerged from the house. "Who's that, Carmine?"

"A spy. The butler hired him to keep an eye on us. Pass it around."

"I never said anything of the kind," Feuermacht argued halfheartedly, happy the workers had accepted his story so easily. He felt sure they'd never confront the butler.

Carmine shoved a box in his hands. "So get to work."

A moment later, Feuermacht entered Le Havre House.

CHAPTER THIRTY-SEVEN

THE COURT OF THE DOMINIONS RARELY ASKED SAINT Peter to appear before them, and when they did, it was usually for matters of universal importance. So it surprised him when a few Dominions summoned him, because they doubted Evangeline could save the President.

I don't understand, Saint Peter reasoned. *What are your specific concerns?*

The rings of the Celestial Hierarchy swirled brilliantly, if momentarily.

Yes. I noticed that, as well. She seems to have lost her spark—second-guessing her every move. But I think she'll rise to the occasion.

The rings circled again.

Will she be able to pull that off without help?

The lights surrounding Saint Peter sizzled.

Of course I'm not questioning the omnipotence of the Hierarchy. It's just that she's having trouble embracing the Collective.

A short burst of light illuminated the heavens.

Yes. I will see that it's done.

Millicent Forsythe had a headache. The caterers, gardeners, and housekeeping staff had pulled her in several different directions to deal with last-minute details. *It's like being drawn and quartered,* she thought as she told everyone to deal with the problems while she took some aspirin and a short nap.

As a result, she didn't know about the afternoon delivery of a leafy, exotic plant in a large box, or that her unhappy decorator had demanded that the staff remove it.

Rather than wreak the ire of Mrs. Forsythe, her butler, Phillips, placed the plant in a storage closet located in back of the ballroom. Few people were aware the space existed. It was wedged between the kitchen and guest bathroom, but led to neither of them. Instead, it contained a dumbwaiter and a trapdoor that opened up to the wine cellar below. The entrance from the ballroom was hidden behind a carved architectural panel that blended into the room's design. Even some of the permanent staff didn't know about the covert closet. Phillips only knew about it because he had once seen Mr. Forsythe disappear into it with one of his paramours, when Millicent got too close for comfort.

Evangeline was so adamant about spying on Bunny that Nigel proposed they split up. It didn't take

Evie long to realize that following Bunny might not be the best use of her time. Bunny spent hours trying on shoes and criticizing each pair. She kept rubbing her feet and complaining to the sales clerk that the linings in the shoes pinched, or were making her feet itchy, or were inferior in some other way. She kept demanding new pairs in different styles and sizes, until she could find something she "could live with."

Although Evangeline had been very particular about her own wardrobe while alive, it had never taken her *this long* to purchase a single pair of shoes. She considered Bunny's shopping excursion frivolous and self-centered. To amuse herself, Evangeline practiced using telekinesis to levitate the shoes Bunny left lying on the floor, back into their boxes. She didn't have much success until she finally moved a single shoe a hair to the right. With that small achievement, she threw herself into the task more wholeheartedly.

Embrace the Collective, she kept thinking to herself. *Embrace the Collective. But don't leave an ectoplasm trail.*

Much to her chagrin, Evangeline was so busy *embracing the Collective*, she didn't notice Bunny's departure. She only realized she had lost her prey when a sales clerk started putting shoes away. Rather than waste time trying to find her, the former spy returned to the hotel to continue practicing telekinesis, out of the view of the living.

Hutch paced outside a Packard show room, with his hands clasped behind his back. He had come to take delivery of a brand-new 1947 Packard Custom Super

Clipper Formal Limousine. It had been made expressly for him, with very particular specifications, and had been sent to a specialty shop near Georgetown to be customized. As soon as he got the call that the work was finished, he rushed to the dealership and told them he needed the car right away, because he was only in town for a day or two and had a special event that evening.

"We haven't picked it up yet from the custom shop, sir. Can you come back in an hour?"

"I'm afraid I can't do that," Hutch replied. "But I've got a better idea. Call the shop and tell them my driver and I are coming in person to pick up the car. I'll just sign all the paperwork here, so I don't have to come back. And, of course, I have a bank check for you to pay for that beauty. I'm pretty sure you'd like to have that right now, wouldn't you?"

"The customer knows best, sir," the manager said, taking the check and handing over the keys. "I'll call them right now and tell them you're on your way."

The sales manager had no way of knowing that Hutch *owned* the custom shop. The industrialist kept his identity buried deep within the legalese used to set up the dummy corporation, which allowed him to make the modifications he wanted without anyone questioning his motives.

John Cullen kept picking at his sleeve. Being called in for questioning by the Commander in Chief of the United States could not be compared to protecting his life. John felt braver about taking a bullet for the President than having to answer the Chief Executive's questions.

At least he didn't have to sit and stew. He got called into the Oval Office right away.

"John." Truman shook the Secret Service agent's hand. "I hear we've got ghosts on the *Ferdinand Magellan*."

John was taken aback by the statement, then realized Frank Wilson had probably told the President what John had said about his pen floating in midair.

"Mr. President, I can't for the life of me figure out what happened onboard that train. But everything I told Frank is true. There were no extraneous personnel on the train, and I would vouch for the honor of every man onboard.

"I don't know of any phenomena that would cause all four tires to go flat at the same time without leaving evidence. I don't know what caused the brake line to fall out, although a tiny hole *was* found in the line. I do know that one of the mechanics who looked at the vehicle says the hole could have caused us to lose our brakes on the ride back to the White House if we had been able to use the car."

"Sounds like *divine intervention* to me."

"I'm glad you have an answer, Mr. President, because I certainly don't."

Left to his own devices, Nigel employed telekinesis to riffle the pages of a tabloid newspaper, looking for a medium. Most of the advertisements seemed too outrageous to be true, but one discreet listing by a Mr. Allwyn Burroughs caught Nigel's attention.

Burroughs's advertisement identified him as an expert in automatic writing. Nigel wanted to send someone a note. But the process would have to be handled in two parts. First, he would have to write instructions for Burroughs. Then, he would have to compose a message for the Secret Service.

Nigel imagined himself at the Wisconsin Avenue address listed in the advertisement, and before he even thought *Deus vult*, he found himself standing in front of a modest brownstone building on a quiet street.

When he arrived at the second-floor walkup, he found it inhabited by an amiable man of massive girth. Nigel collected his thoughts and summoned the powers of the *Collective*. He concentrated on transferring his message to the medium.

It only took a minute for Burroughs to pick up a pen and start scribbling words on a scrap of paper.

When Nigel finished concentrating on the first part of his message, he looked at what the man had written down. The first word stood alone. *Bananas*. It was followed by *Milk*.

Damn! He thought he would try it again when he noticed the confused look on Burroughs's face. Nigel took another look at the list and halfway down the piece of paper saw one of his instructions. *Use your best stationery.*

Burroughs walked over to a tall chinoiserie-style secretary and removed a sheet of plain white paper from one of the drawers. He returned to the table and sat with the pen poised in his hand.

Nigel focused all his thoughts and directed them at the medium, and Burroughs again put pen to paper. He wrote slowly. When he finished, Nigel looked over Burroughs's shoulder to see if his words were clear. The message read:

To the United States Secret Service:

Five years ago, a British MI6 agent was killed in an explosion at the Waldorf Astoria hotel in New York City. That bomb was planted by a woman who is now visiting Washington, D.C.

Her real name is Agatha Strang; however, she has several aliases, including Bunny Stanton, Lady Antonia Southerland, and now, following nuptials to Mr. Hutchinson Reginald Smythe, she is passing herself off as Lady Antonia Southerland Smythe.

She is a fraud and a murderer and is wanted by Interpol as well as your own Federal Bureau of Investigation.

There is reason to believe she may be trying to assassinate President Truman and will be attending a dinner tonight in his honor.

I felt it important that these facts be brought to your attention.

Sincerely,

A concerned citizen

Burroughs had accurately penned Nigel's missive.

The ghost once again compelled the man to write down his words. When Burroughs reached for the stationery, Nigel used telekinesis to move a piece of scrap paper in front of the man.

Thank you, Mr. Burroughs. You are very good at what you do.
        Yours truly,
        Commander Nigel Townsend

Burroughs answered out loud, "I'll see that this gets into the right hands, Commander."

CHAPTER THIRTY-EIGHT

"Have you ever heard of William of Ockham?"

"I don't think so, sir." Frank Wilson was a little confused by the President's question. He had been called back to the Oval Office after the President concluded his interview with John Cullen. "Who is he?"

"The correct question is, who *was* he? William of Ockham was a Franciscan friar who lived in the fourteenth century; a man of logic who believed that when you're trying to determine why something happened, the solution to the problem is the one that makes the fewest assumptions. According to what's known as Ockham's razor, the simplest answer is usually the right one."

"KISS? Keep it simple, stupid?"

Truman grinned. "Yes, Frank, and like KISS and Ockham's razor, I believe in keeping it simple. All of the plausible evidence points to John Cullen. He had opportunity and means. As for motive, maybe he wanted to leave the service in a blaze of glory—by saving the President's life. My life."

"Begging your pardon, Mr. President, but I don't buy it. John doesn't like to be singled out. He's low-key and likes to fade into the background. Grandstanding is not his style."

"Then maybe someone got to him. Maybe he got paid to sabotage the car. Retirement can be expensive."

"And maybe one of the other agents received a payoff to do it. It's an inconclusive argument. And if we have to make the assumption, sir, then it's not in line with Ockham's razor."

"If you're sure that Cullen is guilt-free, I'll accept your finding. But tell me what you've learned about the others. Are they all as equally upstanding?"

Frank shrugged. "Like Cullen, they had opportunity and means, but no motive. I'd bet my reputation that every one of those men is trustworthy beyond fault."

"Are you suggesting we close the investigation?"

"Not at all. I'm suggesting we keep the investigation on the back burner until a future time when new information is revealed to us."

"Okay, Frank. Just tell me one more thing. Who's assigned to my security tonight at the Forsythe party?"

Frank hesitated. "Cullen is, sir, as well as the other men who were assigned to protect you on the *Ferdinand Magellan.*"

"Then maybe you'd like to dust off your tux and

accompany me to this shindig, so we can observe these men in action. We might learn something."

"Of course, sir."

"I hope you have a strong constitution, Frank. Millicent Forsythe's menus favor *rich* food."

"I think I can handle that. And sir?"

"Yes, Frank?"

"If a member of my security team does manage to kill you, I want you to know in advance that I'm very sorry for being so shortsighted. And I regret your passing."

"Not funny."

The afternoon evaporated as Evangeline single-mindedly practiced telekinesis. She found that if she concentrated on a single pinpoint and closed her mind to all outside stimuli, she could move an object a couple of inches, although *slide* might be a better descriptor than *move*.

Before she knew it, it was early evening and she could hear someone banging around in the living room. She found Bunny muttering to herself about the absence of her new husband.

Evangeline waited patiently while Bunny got ready for dinner. When she finished, the new Mrs. Hutchinson Smythe looked very elegant. If Evangeline didn't know better, she would believe the woman standing in front of her really was Lady Antonia Southerland.

Suddenly, the door flew open and Hutch rushed in, larger than life. He gave his wife a peck on the cheek and an empty apology. "Sorry, darling. I got tied up with business. I'll be done in two shakes." Fifteen minutes later, he emerged freshly showered and shaved, tastefully attired in a tuxedo, and ready to take on the evening.

Bunny draped her fur stole around her shoulders. Her stomach rumbled and she grabbed a handful of chocolate bonbons out of the box of candy that she and Hutch had received as a wedding gift. She wrapped them in a handkerchief for the ride to Le Havre House. That should take the edge off her hunger.

Evangeline slipped out with Bunny and Hutch, just the slightest bit annoyed that Nigel was nowhere to be found. She prayed she would be able to follow the couple without his help, and begged the *Collective* for assistance.

Outside Le Havre House, the valet service attending to guests' cars created a strategy to make the retrieval of un-chauffeured vehicles quick and efficient.

Inside the house, Phillips filled tall flutes with champagne and placed them on silver trays laid out across the Carrera marble counters in the butler's pantry. Chefs busied themselves in the kitchen, preparing menu items not already in the ovens or sitting on ice. And a string quartet, hired to provide the evening's entertainment, organized their music in a corner of the ballroom.

Feuermacht helped set tables in the dining room, while making sure he kept his distance from the mistress of the house.

Millicent, dazzling in a gold off-the-shoulder hostess gown that looked like it could have been made for a movie star on the red carpet, checked each table. She couldn't help moving the centerpieces if they were a millimeter out of place and adjusting silverware and napkins until they were perfect.

After he finished setting up, Feuermacht loitered outside the ballroom, waiting for Millicent to leave. The loud ticking of a grandfather clock that stood in the entrance hall echoed throughout the lower floor and the Westminster chimes that marked the quarter hour rang out more than once.

Finally, he heard the click of Millicent's high heels on the hardwood floor and caught sight of her as she headed toward the kitchen.

He needed to make sure everything was ready for that evening, and he didn't want Millicent ruining his plans.

The sound of silence greeted Nigel when he returned to the hotel. He knew the scattered clothing and wet towels meant the Smythes were already on their way to the reception for the President. He willed himself to be reunited with Evangeline and found himself immediately transported to her side.

"Where have you been? I thought I might have to go it alone tonight."

"I had some business to attend to."

She cocked an eyebrow. "How mysterious."

"However, I'm here now. What's going on?"

"Nothing. Yet."

"Let's take a look around."

While they inspected the logistics of the house, it became clear to Nigel they might not be able to adequately protect the President. Even though Le Havre House was a private home, the ballroom had multiple doors and windows that could each contribute to a security breach. Sticking with the President might seem like the best strategy, unless the attack came from a long-range sniper. If Nigel and Evangeline stuck to Bunny and Hutch, they might do some good, unless Feuermacht proved to be the real culprit behind the threat, and Bunny had only been his hired gun at the Imperial Theater. But if they stuck to Feuermacht, and Bunny was the assassin, that, too, could prove fatal. He had no doubt that they would have to split up to do the best job.

The front doorbell chimed with the same deep bass tones of the grandfather clock. Phillips answered the door as Millicent called up to her husband to hurry down, because their guests were arriving.

But it wasn't a guest. John Cullen and some of the other members of the Secret Service detail had been dispatched early, to secure Le Havre House before the President's arrival.

An assistant intercepted Wilson as he left his office and handed him an envelope. "You'll want to take a look at this. It has to do with a woman who may be gunning for the President. It says she's wanted by Interpol. I knew you would want to know more, so I checked the guest list for the Forsythe party and she's a last-minute addition."

"Did you verify the source?"

"Well … it's kind of strange, now that you mention it."

Wilson moaned. "Why can't these things ever be simple and straightforward? What did you find out?"

"The letter is signed *a concerned citizen*. It was delivered by a mountain of a man who says his name is Allwyn Burroughs and claims he can communicate with the dead by writing down their thoughts. I checked, and Mr. Burroughs has lived at the same Georgetown address for the past eleven years. He told me he was asked to deliver the letter to this office by a Commander Nigel Townsend. I checked on him as well. According to Interpol, he died eight years ago."

Wilson stared at his assistant. The whole thing sounded preposterous. But so did the mystery surrounding the sabotage of the President's car. Was he supposed to believe he was getting help *from the other side*?

He took the letter. "I guess we'll keep an eye open for this Bunny Stanton woman. Who did you say she was—Mrs. Hutchinson Smythe? That would be an interesting turn of events. A man who's morally bankrupt married to a woman who's a fraud."

"A woman who's a fraud, who may be trying to kill the President."

"Thanks for reminding me."

John stationed only two members of his team indoors. He placed three men outside the French doors leading to the ballroom, two more near the front door, and a sixth man at the entrance gate to the property.

Following the debacle onboard the *Ferdinand Magellan*, Cullen had instructions to "remove the President to safety" at even the smallest disturbance. Secret Service director Frank Wilson made it clear that the department would take no chances. Frank would personally escort the President and First Lady to the Forsythes' gala.

At the stroke of eight, the string quartet began

playing a selection from Vivaldi's *Four Seasons*.

The first of many cars rolled up to the front door to drop off invited guests. Millicent's husband descended the steps, ready to embrace the evening and some of the more comely females in attendance. And behind the closed door of a storage closet in the far corner of the ballroom, a plant began making odd ticking sounds that no one could hear.

EG.

CHAPTER THIRTY-NINE

Bunny played with the chocolates clutched in her hand. She wanted to eat them, but didn't want to have candy stuck to her teeth when she greeted her hosts at the party. Finally, she folded the handkerchief over them and thrust the packet into her bag. *Maybe later.*

The President's Lincoln pulled up in front of Le Havre House just moments after the security team gave his driver the all-clear sign. Truman planned to be on the receiving line so he could personally greet Millicent's guests and see for himself if any of them had a nefarious glint in their eye. He counted on the other guests arriving fashionably late, and he was right on the money. He was the first to arrive.

Phillips escorted the President, the First Lady, and Frank Wilson to the ballroom, where Millicent and

Gregory Forsythe greeted them.

"It's good to see our Commander in Chief is a man who takes punctuality seriously," Gregory said. "I, myself, have been known to arrive late every now and again for various events, sir, and I'm chastened by the ability of the most important man in America to show up at my house for dinner exactly at the appointed hour."

"Don't pay any attention to him, Mr. President," Millicent said as she took Truman's hand. "I'm told you would like to be part of the receiving line, and I graciously accept your offer."

The words were no sooner said when the Italian ambassador arrived.

"Let the festivities begin," Wilson said, just loud enough for the President to hear.

Soon, a steady stream of Washington power brokers and their wives stood waiting to greet the President and First Lady and their gracious hosts.

A brand-new black-and-pearl-gray 1947 Packard limousine rolled through the entry of Le Havre House. Its uniformed chauffeur opened the door for Mr. and Mrs. Hutchinson Smythe and helped them out of the vehicle.

Bunny studied the house, trying not to look as if she were gaping. It was the kind of place where she envisioned herself living with Hutch. She wondered if the Forsythes would be interested in selling it.

"You can park at the end of the row," one of the valets told Hutch's chauffeur, while he gestured with his arm toward the far end of the field.

"You know, if this baby gets scratched," the

chauffeur replied, "I'll get my head handed to me. She's only a few hours old. What would you say if I drove her over to the entry gate and parked under that tree?" He slipped the valet a twenty-dollar bill. "Mr. Smythe would really appreciate it if we take care of his car."

Twenty dollars. It was more than the valet would receive for the entire night on the job. Maybe more than he would make all weekend. "Sure thing!" he said with a big smile. "Park her anywhere you like."

Feuermacht noted Bunny's arrival with a modicum of disappointment. He had hoped she would have eaten herself into oblivion by now. But aside from an obvious flush, she seemed as healthy as an ox.

He couldn't understand what the problem was. For a second, he wondered if she could be in love. *Love? Bunny? No.* As far as he was concerned, she was jaded, cold, and calculating and not likely to succumb to bourgeois rituals like marriage unless it promised a payoff.

Of course, Smythe was one of the richest men in America, if not the world, and that was a pretty big payoff. *Could she know the candy is poisoned?* He had far too high an opinion of himself and his talents to think she was smart enough to figure that out on her own.

Patience, he told himself. *All things come to those who wait.*

As Wilson savored his first sip of twenty-year-old Glenfiddich single-malt scotch, an agent posted near the door inclined his head toward an attractive brunette, who hung on the arm of Hutchinson Smythe. She didn't look like an *assassin* or a *confidence woman*, but Wilson couldn't take any chances. He nodded to the agent, who began observing her every move.

Bunny couldn't stop thinking about the chocolate bonbons. The more she thought about them, the more she wanted them. It didn't matter that she was surrounded by some of the most important people in the world—eating exquisite hors d'oeuvres. She wanted a piece of candy.

She looked around and when she thought no one was watching, she popped one of the bonbons in her mouth. The chocolate soothed her. The flavor of almonds reminded her of her favorite liqueur. The candy had another flavor that she couldn't quite figure out, but it didn't matter. She needed to eat just one more piece.

Nigel poked his nose into every nook and cranny on the main floor of Le Havre House, looking for something amiss. He had already watched in horror as the caterers filled a top-shelf liquor bottle with a decidedly inferior gin. And he marveled at how little caviar actually made its way onto the canapés.

He extended his search, checking every room of the house, under beds and in bathrooms. He had always been amazed at some of the odd things people had hidden away behind closed doors, and would have been indulging his voyeuristic streak if the President's safety were not at stake. But he took this particular search seriously, and while he sensed something was amiss, he just couldn't see it.

Evangeline did a double take when she spotted

Feuermacht working at the party. She figured he was up to no good and kept her eye on him. Just his presence there was enough to rouse her suspicion, but after an hour, all he had done was serve cocktails and remove empty glasses.

Suddenly Feuermacht stopped in his tracks and a small smile played upon his lips. Evangeline followed his gaze and saw that he was staring at Bunny. They both watched as Bunny took a chocolate bonbon from her handkerchief and popped it into her mouth.

"No. No. No," her husband chortled as he snatched the rest of the candy out of Bunny's hand and stuffed it into his jacket pocket. "I can't have my new wife losing her girlish figure so early in our marriage."

Evangeline looked back at Feuermacht. His smile had disappeared. He abruptly turned and stormed into the kitchen. She followed him just in time to see him pick up a carving knife and return with it to the ballroom.

CHAPTER FORTY

"Try some caviar," Hutch told his wife as he took two canapés from a tray. He studied them for a moment and lowered his voice. "If you can find it."

"I can't eat caviar with the taste of chocolate in my mouth."

"Exactly. Go rinse your mouth out so you can savor the salty sweetness of beluga."

Bunny sighed and walked away as Hutch stuffed both canapés in his mouth.

One of his business partners stood nearby. Marshall Maximilian Montague was a key player in the Smythe family's South African mining operations. Montague had been lobbying D.C. officials to ease up on attempts to join with other nations to regulate mining operations. He approached Hutch right after Bunny left.

"I didn't realize you knew Bunny." Montague

C. A. PACK

nodded at the retreating Mrs. Smythe.

"What are you talking about?"

"Bunny Stanton. The woman you were just talking to."

"You'd better get your eyes checked, pal. The woman who just left here is my wife."

"Your wife!"

"Lady Antonia Southerland Smythe. She should be able to open a few doors for us with the British government."

"You've been had, my friend. The woman I just saw you with is Bunny Stanton, and that's a fact. She hires out for sticky jobs, like erasing mistakes. I hired her to take care of our big problem."

"WHAT?" The color of Hutch's face changed from white to red to purple.

The Secret Service agent who had been spying on Bunny observed Hutch and Montague since he couldn't easily follow Bunny into the powder room. He witnessed the men's conversation and almost immediately began whispering into a walkie-talkie. He stated a third party had just confirmed the identity of a woman the Secret Service had under observation. She used an assumed name and could be a mercenary-for-hire. It was time to evacuate the President.

Anyone standing near Frank Wilson heard him grinding his teeth as he listened to the agent's report. Wilson had accompanied the President in case something out-of-the-way happened, but all he really hoped for was a quiet night with good food. Visions of filet mignon danced in his head, but would not be heading down to his stomach. "I'll corral the President," he told the agent. "You call for the car." He sighed. "Have it pick us up out front." He grabbed John Cullen and told him to find the First Lady and tell her that they had to leave quickly but discreetly.

Wilson did not need to wait long for an opportune moment to intercept the President. Truman had just finished telling an anecdote to a small group of bipartisan lawmakers and had excused himself as they laughed politely. He walked over to Wilson. "You've got an odd look on your face, Frank."

"We need to leave, Mr. President. Le Havre House is no longer secure."

"The First Lady …"

"Cullen is with her." Wilson nodded toward the front door. "If I'm not mistaken, she's saying good night to our hostess."

"Well, then, let's follow her lead." Truman made his way to the door, nodding politely to people he didn't know well and shaking hands with those he did, while never breaking his stride.

Montague watched as Hutch took a handkerchief out of his pocket and started angrily stuffing bonbons into his mouth.

Hutch was livid. "I hired my own man to do the job. Someone named Faust. But he's done damn near nothing as far as I can tell, so I've taken matters into my own hands."

"I can't believe you took that chance. I told you I would take care of it. If this guy knows who you are, the whole thing may quite possibly blow up in your face."

"What can he do? He doesn't know who hired him. It was done anonymously."

"Thank God for small favors."

God's got nothing to do with this, Saint Peter thought as he observed the action at the Forsythe party. Evangeline and Nigel were about to be put to the test.

Where are they, anyway?

Hutch's chauffeur saw the President's car head up to the house. That was his cue. He casually walked around the Packard and opened the trunk, laying his jacket inside. While he was at it, he switched on the timer to a bomb that had been custom built into the vehicle.

The chauffeur walked away from the Packard and headed over to where the other drivers were waiting for their passengers. "Any of you gentlemen got a Chesterfield? I'm all out and I'm dying for a smoke."

Montague knew when it was time to cut loose and run. He had known Hutchinson Smythe for years, and the man was a hotheaded risk taker.

"See you later, Hutch," he said as he left. He escaped to his new Maserati A6 Pininfarina Berlinetta; a classy-looking sports car with a long hood and a chrome grill, but more than looks, it had power. Montague counted on it to quickly whisk him away.

As he turned the key in the ignition, he saw the gate to Le Havre House open. *Someone's leaving,* he thought. He gunned the car so he would get there before it closed. He didn't want to waste a single moment of time waiting for the guard to reopen the gate just for him. He never anticipated a car carrying the French Ambassador would enter from the other side.

The sound of splintering metal carried in the still night air as the two vehicles collided at the gate, blocking it.

It only took the President a moment to soothe Millicent Forsythe's ruffled feathers when she heard he was leaving before dinner. He explained it was a matter of national security and eased her disappointment by promising to invite her to dinner at the White House.

He reached for his wife's arm and made a gracious exit, with Frank Wilson following closely on their heels.

Once they were safely inside the Lincoln, Frank heaved a sigh of relief. However, they only traveled as far as the gate. Montague's mangled Maserati blocked the exit.

After checking all the rooms in Le Havre House, Nigel returned to the ballroom. *There has to be something here, something that I'm missing.* He circled the room, looking for anything that seemed out of place.

He was in the far corner of the room when the string quartet came to the end of a sonata. In the ensuing moment of silence, Nigel heard ticking.

Evangeline followed Feuermacht out of the kitchen. She looked around for Nigel and spotted him in a corner of the ballroom, inspecting the walls. She called out his name, but got no reaction. She wanted Nigel's help, but refused to leave Feuermacht's side. She was too afraid of whom he might hurt with the knife.

***

Bunny returned from rinsing out her mouth, and Hutch practically assaulted her.

"Darling, who's Bunny Stanton?" he hissed.

Bunny blanched. His words left her speechless.

Hutch grabbed her arm and twisted it until she winced with pain. "Come with me, dearest," he grumbled.

Bunny knocked into him, kicking him as hard as she could. When he lifted his knee to clutch his sore shin, she hooked her foot behind his other leg and shoved him off balance. She quickly strode away—pushing her way though an astonished group of onlookers—and sought refuge by locking herself in the bathroom.

Feuermacht made a beeline for Bunny with the knife in his hand, until he saw her confrontation with Hutch. If Smythe wanted to do his dirty work, Feuermacht was more than happy to let him. He turned toward the sideboard, where a filet of beef sat on a silver platter, and plunged the knife into it.

Nigel popped his head inside the wall of the secret storage closet. Not even a foot away, he discovered a homemade bomb ticking away inside a planter. He summoned whatever power he could from the *Collective* to help him shut it down, but almost instantly knew it was futile. The ticking had stopped.

The bomb exploded, sending a fireball of flames into the ballroom and blowing out the wall to the bathroom where Bunny hid.

EG

CHAPTER FORTY-ONE

THE EXPLOSION ROCKED THE BALLROOM, REPLACING classical music with a symphony of guests' screams. People nearest the French doors escaped outside, upset but unscathed. However, those standing nearest the explosive device were showered with fiery debris. One man became trapped under what had been the secret door to the storage closet. The percussion from the blast had ripped the carved panel off its hinges and sent it flying. He was rescued by a musician who yanked the flaming door off the stunned and bloodied victim and helped him to safety.

The adjacent bathroom suffered worse damage. A massive 19th-century Italian rococo mirror had blown off the wall, crushing Bunny beneath it. The force of the impact rendered her unconscious. Bunny lay motionless as flames licked at the mirror's ornate frame, causing the gold-leaf finish to bubble and burn. A trickle of her blood, unleashed by the splintered glass, crept across the white marble floor.

Hutch had been knocked off his feet. He was stunned, but otherwise unharmed.

Nearby, one of the female guests screamed hysterically as she swatted at the flames that were eating away her dress. A diplomat pulled off his jacket and used it to smother the smoldering ball gown, then helped the weeping woman to safety.

Hutch couldn't be bothered with heroics. He needed to get outside. But instead of joining the other guests in the back gardens, he made his way to the front of the house, hoping he wasn't too late to witness the surprise he had planned for the President.

"Is there any way around it?" Frank Wilson didn't like the idea of the President being stuck on the ground of Le Havre House. He had gotten word from his agents that there had been an explosion inside the home and several people were injured. "We're like sitting ducks out here."

"What caused the explosion, Frank? You didn't say." The President obviously wanted to know what was going on.

"We're not sure yet. Our men are helping with the injured and emergency vehicles are being dispatched. But I don't like it. First of all, how are they going to get in when we can't get out? Secondly, who's to say some unauthorized personnel won't sneak in with the emergency workers?"

"What do you suggest we do, then?"

"Nothing, sir. Absolutely nothing. We're safer in here than we are out there." A second-story window exploded, punctuating Wilson's point.

A short distance away, valets and chauffeurs stared at the blazing home, mesmerized by the unbelievable turn of events.

Feuermacht's heart pounded and his adrenaline surged. He didn't see Bunny anywhere and thought maybe he had gotten rid of her for good.

He wanted to leave, but knew he had better stay put. Appearances meant everything. It would look much better if he helped with the injured than if he were spotted scurrying away. *That* would make him look guilty, and that's the last thing he needed.

He walked among the injured guests and tried to console those who were alone and crying. *This should look good to anyone who's observing me.*

Saint Peter stepped away from the *Collective*. A decision had been made that he knew would upset the apple cart. He hadn't seen it coming, but the *Collective* was right, of course. It was time.

A final breath escaped from beneath the rococo mirror.

Instantaneously, a well-dressed brunette beyond the first blush of youth appeared at the end of one of the lines to the Pearly Gates. She seemed bewildered, just like so many others who found their way there.

Saint Peter sighed. He knew Bunny would try to turn his little piece of Heaven into Hell personified when she figured out what had happened.

Nigel Townsend suddenly appeared at the head of another line. *What did I do now?* he wondered.

Nothing, an angel answered telepathically. *You did not disarm the bomb. Agatha Strang, whom you know as Bunny, was killed in the explosion. Your death has been avenged by the demise of your murderer.*

But what about Evie?

Evangeline must do what she is meant to do.

Evangeline suddenly went cold. She instinctively knew Nigel was gone. She didn't need to see it happen. She sensed his change of status in the *Collective*. In a way, she could still feel his influence and was aware of his thoughts.

You can do it, Evie. But you'll have to do it on your own.

CHAPTER FORTY-TWO

EVANGELINE POPPED INTO THE PRESIDENT'S LINCOLN
to make sure he was safe and sound. His car remained
immobilized because of Montague's accident, but
Truman and the other passengers appeared to be okay. If
she could speed up Montague's departure, the President
could return to the relative safety of the White House.

She left the grounds to investigate the accident.
The French Ambassador's chauffeur suffered broken
ribs and internal bleeding. An ambulance took him to
a nearby hospital. The Ambassador wasn't as badly hurt.
He had a broken nose and a nasty bump on his head.
That was the extent of the injuries to the occupants of his
limousine.

Montague had not fared as well. He was strapped
onto a gurney, but his medical team did not move as fast
as the other medics. As Evangeline moved closer, she

sensed the presence of the *Collective*—not for herself but for Montague. She could already imagine him in the next dimension, not quite sure of what had happened.

Then she saw a ghost. If she had a beating heart, it would have stopped. The apparition looked like Christian Butler, her former partner, but he disappeared before she could reach him. She'd have to look for him later.

A private tow-truck operator fastened a hook to Montague's Maserati, so it could be moved out of the way.

That's good, thought Evangeline. *Once that's gone, the President's car will be able to squeeze by.*

Bunny was too dazed to argue with Saint Peter when he told her to get on line six.

"Six?" she muttered.

"Yes, six. Rhymes with the River Styx—which is paved with good intentions."

She just shook her head.

Saint Peter pointed in the general direction, but Bunny stood rooted to the spot. She was still trying to make sense of what happened when an angel led her away.

Nigel observed Bunny's dilemma from several lines away. In a small way, he felt sorry for her. But that was in a *very* small way. She had created hell on earth for some people, and now she was en route to the real thing.

Nigel, on the other hand, was earmarked for Heaven. He was surprised by the decision. It seems he was credited as a humanitarian, rather than a killing machine, for his work with the British Secret Service. He'd been worried about that. Now, he wasn't sure he would be right for Heaven. He waited on line to seek an audience with the *Collective*, to see if his talents might be put to better use. As long as the Celestial Hierarchy continued to allow sentient beings to have free will, there would be a need for souls like Nigel to help set things to right.

Hutch stood in front of Le Havre House, staring through bloodshot eyes at pandemonium—fueled by politicos fleeing the Forsythe inferno. But that's not what interested him. He was waiting for his car to explode, and didn't know why it was taking longer than expected. He feared the President's limo would pull away before his scheme to eliminate his biggest detractor could get off the ground.

The President has no right trying to regulate mining on the other side of the world. It's out of his jurisdiction. He's a megalomaniac who must be stopped. Without him, attempts by the other European nations will fall apart. The status quo for the Smythe Industrial Conglomerate will be maintained.

He closed his eyes. *I must be coming down with the flu.* His head felt too heavy for his neck to support. Even his shoulders ached. As if that weren't enough, his stomach roiled. *Or maybe it's the caviar.* He felt himself heave. He ducked behind some bushes just as the first wave of nausea hit him full force, and he left his mark on the Forsythes' lawn.

Millicent Forsythe could hardly believe the unfolding drama. Her party was ruined. Her house was on fire, blazing out of control. And her reputation was in a shambles. Her husband, Gregory, had mortgaged the property to the hilt to finance a business venture that had failed. Now, they would be left with nothing.

Fire trucks had aggregated outside the front gate, waiting for the car accident to be cleared away so they could gain access to the property.

Millicent wanted her husband to tell them about a little-used service entrance around back. There were a few shrubberies planted inside the chain-link gate to mask its utilitarian appearance, but it would be easy for the trucks to just drive right over them. *Where the hell is Gregory?*

She removed her high heels so she could walk more easily on the grass, and headed toward the front of the house to look for her husband. She shuddered when she saw Hutchinson Smythe retching in the bushes.

Another set of windows blew out as the small canisters of gas in the caterer's portable stoves exploded. That made her break into a trot, but she stopped short when she saw her husband leaning against a tree, fondling his mistress. Her life had gone from heaven to hell within a few minutes, and she could feel hot tears starting to stream down her face.

"Oh, Gregory," his mistress moaned as he dropped to his knees. Millicent watched her husband's head disappear under the other woman's dress.

But that was nothing compared to what happened next.

EG

CHAPTER FORTY-THREE

BOOM!

Hutch's limousine blew apart, sending wreckage in every direction. Shrapnel and molten pitch pierced Evangeline's essence, momentarily unsettling her. She came to her senses when she realized the President's car had been idling right next to the limo that blew up. Her spirit manifested inside the burning vehicle, which had flipped over.

The force of the blast had knocked out the President and his companions. She would have to find a way to move them to safety.

Secret Service agents rushed to the smoldering car. It was covered with a fiery tar coating that had sprayed out of the exploding limo. The agents risked their own skin as they fought to get to the President, but the doors resisted their efforts to pry them open. The President's car was built like a tank and locked tight as a drum. One G-man picked up a rock and smashed it against the windshield, but the glass was a special composite material bonded to plastic, making it strong enough for military applications—like protecting the President of the United States.

Unless they could get the occupants out of the vehicle, all the passengers, including the Commander in Chief, would roast to death like suckling pigs on a spit.

Evangeline did her best, but could not move President Truman out of the burning vehicle. Her attempts to use telekinesis to open the locks were useless. She *tried* to embrace the *Collective*, but the *Collective* wouldn't embrace her back. She could feel herself becoming frustrated. The more panic she felt, the harder she tried, but nothing worked for her. If only she had stayed with the President instead of going to look at Montague's accident, she might have been able to do some good. Instead, she had made a wrong decision, and the victim would be America's First Citizen.

She wished she could go back in time for just one minute, but Nigel had never explained to her how he had done that. *God help me.*

Evangeline suddenly found herself transported back in time. She was inside the President's car as it pulled away from Le Havre House. Without a moment's hesitation, she embraced the *Collective* and grabbed the steering wheel. She wrenched it to one side, causing the car to veer off the driveway and into some bushes.

"Goodness gracious," Bess Truman uttered as she was thrown forward.

"What's going on here?" the President demanded.

"Watch where you're going," Wilson chastised the driver.

"I don't know what happened, sir. It's like the car has a mind of its own."

"Is anyone hurt?" Wilson asked.

"Bess, are you all right?" the President inquired as he helped his wife up. The First Lady had slid off the seat when the car stopped short.

"I'm just a little shook up."

BOOM!

"My God, would you look at that!"

Not too far away, Hutch's car had exploded, spewing flaming debris everywhere. Sparks showered the President's car, burning the paint finish, but Wilson would not allow anyone to leave the vehicle until backup arrived.

"Do you realize that if your driver hadn't veered off the road, we might have been right next to that car when it blew up?" The First Lady's question made the hairs on the back of Wilson's neck stand on end.

"The funniest thing, Frank," the President said, "I could swear I saw that pesky poltergeist tugging at our steering wheel, causing us to run into these bushes. But in retrospect, I think I was right when I joked that it was divine intervention. I think it was an angel."

"You're not joking now, are you, sir? Because I think I saw something, too—the wispy outline of a woman. But just for a moment. And then it was gone."

"Regardless of whether it was a ghost or an angel, I'm just glad she was here," Bess Truman interjected. "Or else the *Veep* would be giving 'em hell, Harry, instead of you."

Moments later, a phalanx of government, police, and military personnel converged on the Forsythe grounds through the rear entrance.

"So, Frank," the President asked, "off the record, are we saying maybe she's the same angel who disabled my car on the *Ferdinand Magellan*?"

"I can't say, Mr. President. There are still a lot of unanswered questions."

"Like why that limousine over there blew up?"

"And why the Forsythes' house is on fire," the First Lady said, as a fire truck drove through the entrance gate toward Le Havre House.

"It looks like I'm going to have a long night ahead of me. I'd better get out here. You should be fine without me, Mr. President. You have an angel watching over you. Good night Mrs. Truman. Stay safe."

Frank stopped by the driver's window and motioned for him to roll it down. "Take the First Family directly home. Don't stop for anything. If there's a problem, drive around it. Just wait a moment for me to rustle up a couple of cars to escort you back to the White House."

Evangeline exited the President's car. They had seen her. There would be hell to pay. She shuddered at the thought.

From her vantage point on the lawn, she could see the flames from the multiple explosions reflected in the windows of the President's Lincoln.

Feuermacht watched as officials removed Bunny's

remains from Le Havre House. At least one of his projects had reached fruition. Of course, he had failed to kill the President, but he wasn't really worried about that. He would tell whoever hired him that he had rigged one of the explosions.

He watched Hutch vomit in the bushes not too far away, and felt a sense of accomplishment that his poison had claimed a victim. An emergency worker grabbed Hutch's arm and led him to a waiting ambulance.

Feuermacht knew it was time to leave. He turned back to the house for a last look and saw one of the caterers speaking animatedly with police. He watched as the man pointed him out and the officer started walking toward him. *Stay calm. Stay cool. They have nothing on me.* "Good evening, Officer. May I be of assistance?"

"Are you Sebastian Faust?"

"Yes." Feuermacht offered to shake the officer's hand.

In return, the cop slapped a handcuff around Feuermacht's wrist. "You're under arrest, Mr. Faust. You were observed acting suspiciously by officials in New York and here in Washington, and a subsequent search of your hotel room has turned up a few interesting articles."

"What is the charge, may I ask?"

"Attempted murder of the President of the United States, possession of a deadly substance, destruction of property—need I go on?"

Saint Peter had been taking time out from his duties at the Pearly Gates to observe Evangeline's big moment.

Good call on that one, right? He silently addressed

the *Collective. Maybe we should recruit her into U1?*

She's not ready for that.

How about MWG? Saint Peter countered.

Narrow it down.

Saint Peter nearly slapped the side of his head with the flat of his hand when he suddenly realized the Celestial Hierarchy and the *Collective* would not accept anything outside of Evangeline's current sphere of understanding. *MWG-OASS-3?*

She may be able to do some good there while she's working to rest in peace.

I think earth may be way too small to hold her, now that she's seen the bright lights of the Collective.

She's still a neophyte and needs guidance.

Then Milky Way Galaxy, Orion's Arm Solar System, planet Earth it is. Saint Peter knew how to quit while he was ahead.

Evangeline continued to watch from the sideline. *Mission accomplished.* She had saved the President's life. She knew she couldn't have done it without the *Collective's* help. She felt like she had been a part of something good, but now she'd have to pay the piper.

A moment later, Saint Peter stood by her side.

"They saw me. I couldn't help it. What line should I get on when we get back?"

Saint Peter laughed. Evangeline's attitude had made a 180-degree adjustment.

We've decided to let that slide.

She could hear him, even though his lips didn't move.

Is this what being part of the Collective is like? she

wondered.

Yes, and I'm glad to see you're embracing us.

Not sure he could understand her, she continued to speak out loud. "While we're embracing, would you like to tell me how Siegfried Feuermacht rose from the dead?"

Why does his name sound so familiar?

"Because you promised me that you'd check to see whether he was actually dead."

That's right. I looked up that information for you. He reached into his pocket and pulled out a wadded-up piece of parchment and flattened it out. *He's not dead. The Nazis shot his illegally cloned duplicate.*

"I don't know what that means."

Feuermacht took part in a secret scientific experiment to create an exact duplicate of himself, following Germany's defeat in the Great War. It worked, and within a decade, an exact replica of Feuermacht walked the earth until the Nazis executed him, thinking he was Feuermacht. We weren't quite sure what to do with him when he arrived at the Gates, so we put him to work in the archives. Anyway, the short answer to your question is, Siegfried Feuermacht is alive.

"So now what?" Nigel was gone. She knew she would miss him a lot, even though she had the *Collective* keeping her company and Nigel, in theory, was part of the *Collective*.

Well, you returned to earth to avenge your murder, but it may turn out to be a never-ending task unless I give you a little hint.

"What's the hint?"

Ruth Peters.

"Who is that?"

Sorry. That's all I can tell you.

"But I don't understand. Is she the one who killed me? Or is she someone who can help me find my killer?"

I can see you don't understand the meaning of "that's all I can tell you." Should I say it in French? Would that help? C'est tout que je peux dire. I just love the way that rolls off my tongue.

"Why are you joking about this? I can't believe a saint even knows how to joke."

Hey, saints are human. Not like angels—who, I might add, have absolutely no sense of humor.

"All right. I get it. I'm on my own."

Maybe not for long.

"What do you mean?"

Saint Peter winked. *I've got a proposition for you that I think you're going to love.*

Excerpt from:
EVANGELINE'S GHOST:
HOUDINI

Everything was status quo back at the Pearly Gates.

Saint Peter was dispensing destinies at the head of Line One, when he spotted Evangeline trailing a heavenly document a quarter-mile long.

Ethereal treatises were usually lighter than gossamer because they automatically scrolled as the words changed. But the Celestial Hierarchy had unanimously ruled that Evangeline's incident report should be more than a mere collection of her extracted memories. Instead, they told her to document the attempted assassination of President Truman *for the archives*. Her instructions: to include complete lists of all people involved and their histories; all locations involved—including maps, specs and blueprints; and a second-by-second description of Evangeline's every thought, action, and reaction from the moment she first arrived at the Pearly Gates to the moment she began archiving what happened. She also created an index and a complete, but short, synopsis for beings who did not want to read the entire debriefing. The result was the epitome of minutia.

They were testing her and every soul knew it, including Evangeline. It was an experiment to see if she would embellish the truth or withhold information. The *Collective* believed *bad habits are hard to break* and they wanted to make sure Evangeline was right for MWG-OA-SS3.

The MWG-OA-SS3—part of the USSA, or Universal Secret Service Agency—was code for Milky Way Galaxy: Orion Arm: Solar System: Third Planet; or as Evangeline and Saint Peter knew it, Earth. It had been Evangeline's home when she was alive and would serve as her home base now that she was dead, but not gone.

The incident report, instead of being on a filmy piece of gossamer, was on a heavy parchment scroll that had unwound to more than thirteen hundred feet in length. And some of the newer souls, who were not quite sure where they were yet, kept tripping over it and in some cases, falling down.

Saint Peter called for a battalion of angels to stand guard over their flocks and help displaced spirits climb over or detour around the snaking parchment.

"There's got to be a better way to do this," Evangeline complained to Saint Peter. "For a group of beings who know my every thought even before I think it, I find this sort of red tape unproductive and archaic."

Heaven is a very old place, he answered telepathically. *What you think of as 'archaic,' the Collective thinks of* as 'time-tested.' And what you call 'unproductive,' the 'big C' believes is 'good business practice.' Am I to assume by your very presence here that you have completed your paperwork?

"I have, except for one point. There was a time when I was standing outside Le Havre House, when I caught a momentary glimpse of a man I thought I knew. His name is, or was, Christian Butler. He used to be an operative for MI6 as well as a Wing Commander for the Royal Air Force.

"Now in section 92D, part A, paragraph 17, clause 62, it asks me to name all the people I saw standing on the grounds of Le Havre House on the night of the explosion. But you see, I don't want to add Christian's name to the document, if he wasn't there. Would you happen to know, for certain, if Christian was there?"

That is such a really great name, don't you agree? Up here at the Pearly Gates, we like names like Christian, Angelique, and even Evangeline if you must know, but don't let it go to your head.

"You didn't answer my question."

What are you, a barrister? Did you graduate from law school when I wasn't looking? You may not have noticed this, but I outrank you. And in many situations, what you just said would be considered insubordination. Do you know what happens to souls who are insubordinate? I shudder to even think about it. A mild rumble of thunder reverberated around them.

"You still haven't answered my question."

YES! Yes. Yes, it was Christian Butler. What's it to you?

"Why was he there?"

Why are any souls roaming around on Earth past

their expiration date? He's out to avenge his death.

"But the man responsible for his death died on the same day. He was a Kamikaze pilot who crashed his plane into the aircraft carrier that Christian was assigned to. Why would Christian need to avenge his death?"

You are two of a kind! Your friend's argument was that the man who ordered his death is not the same person—as the man who died. He's looking for the officer who ordered the pilot to crash into his ship. That's not going to be easy for him to prove.

"Maybe we could work together? I bet I could help him. And he could help me."

I'm onto your game, missy. I know the two of you knew each other in the biblical sense. And now that Nigel Townsend has gone to meet his maker, you're looking for a new toe-curler.

Evangeline felt herself blush. She hoped that being dead would help mask it, but she saw Saint Peter smirk.

At least we wish he had gone to meet his maker, Saint Peter continued. *Townsend seems to think he should be part of the USS on a permanent basis. But that's none of your concern. Why can't you people understand that's not how the Collective works?*

"I'm not interested in Nigel, right now. I'm interested in Christian."

Ooh …Fickle!

"I'm not fickle. I was just asking if I could work with Christian. Is there someone I should see, besides you, to find out if that's possible?"

Line seven hundred seventy-seven. "Next!"

ACKNOWLEDGEMENTS

Thanks to my family and friends who managed not to hate me during my incessant social media posts about each individual chapter being written.

Writing Evangeline's Ghost would not have been possible without my husband Andrew's support, as well as the well-wishes of my former newsroom colleagues. And a fond shout out to my pals Barbara Paskoff and Carol Scibelli who have somehow remained my friends, even though I've become a literal recluse.

Special thanks to editor Neil Hock, who made sure my i's were dotted and my t's were crossed, and to Karen Dionne for her advice and inspiration.

And a big hug for Joann Colucci for her constant encouragement throughout my writing process.

ABOUT THE AUTHOR

C. A. Pack is an award-winning journalist, and former assignment manager/anchor at *LI News Tonight* in New York. She has worked as a news writer at WNBC-TV, and Cablevision's News 12 Long Island. She also created/produced a pilot for a proposed special-interest television series called *The Wedding Show* for the PAX network.

Now, Carol has switched her focus from fact to fiction.

She is currently at work on her fourth novel featuring Evangeline, and she is also busy writing the next exciting segment of the *Library of Illumination* series, which will soon be published as *The First Chronicles of Illumination,* a YA fantasy.

A current member of International ThrillerWriters, and Sisters in Crime, Carol is also a former president of the Press Club of Long Island. She lives in Westbury, NY, with her husband, a couple of picky parrots, and dozens of imaginary characters who are constantly demanding page space.